MW01138791

After the Storm

Book 2

"Boston"

By

Don Chase

This is a work of fiction. All characters appearing in this work are fictitious. Any resemblance to real persons, living or dead, is purely coincidental. Organizations and events portrayed in this story are either products of the author's imagination or are used fictitiously.

For Rodney, Matt and Glenn,

Thanks for all the help, advice and support.

Prologue

This one will be shorter, I promise.

The world as we know it is no more. A giant meteor hit the US five years ago, turning a good portion of it into a desolate wasteland. Between the meteor, the nuclear winter that followed and the rioting, it wiped out almost 95% of the population. The government went into hiding and left the remaining population to fend for itself for over two years.

Almost three years after the "Storm" the government came out of their bunkers, the leadership had changed drastically though. The men who had run the country before have since died and the man in charge had been the Secretary of housing and urban development in the previous administration. He was not suited, nor did he necessarily want the job of president but he was in the line of succession and thusly they looked to him for leadership. Leadership was in no way his strong suit.

Five years after the "Storm" and the remaining populace have had to fight to survive. Many have lost their lives in the subsequent days and those that remain, stand together and take care of each other, "Clans" have formed where there used to be towns and they are governed by a clan "head" or "chief". Duncan Mackenzie is one of these clan heads in a small town just outside what's left of Boston, Massachusetts. He and his men find food, water and supplies to keep the rest of the 1000 plus members of his clan alive, anyway they can. This includes foraging, bartering with other clans or if they have to, stealing it from what remains of the old government.

Recently, the government has taken a renewed interest in the Boston area clans. They've come under new command led by Colonel Jacobson who was sent here to whip the clans into line. The military had once again set up a camp in our little town of Menotomy and begun operations centered on either silencing or destroying us. I'm not actually sure which it is at this point. They have ambushed us and kidnapped our doctors, one of which is my wife Chris. The doctors and my wife have all been rescued safely and the camp was destroyed. During all of this, I discovered it wasn't the army's intention to destroy our clan at all. From what I've been told by a now dead captain was that it was me that was being hunted not the clan. Somehow, I made it onto Colonel Jacobson's wish list. Now all I need to do is figure out why and how to avoid being his next birthday present.

Chapter 1

The sun was shining and I could feel the breeze blowing lightly through my hair. I was sitting on the back steps of our house watching Justin throw his baseball straight up in the air. He was trying to catch it in his brand new glove that we had gotten him yesterday for his fifth birthday. Lily was scampering around the yard sniffing at this and that. It was early summer and the grass was green and the birds were chirping as the traffic rumbled along in front of the house. Finally, Justin caught one.

"Dad, Dad I got it! I got it!" he yelled as he ran toward me waving the glove around over his head.

I smiled and said "Good work buddy!" as I clapped for him.

I laughed as I watched him dance around while Lily circled him. She barked happily thinking that they were playing some kind of game. His light brown hair was short and tousled. He had huge doe like dark brown eyes and Chris' smile. He made me happy every day. My heart sang as I watched him jump around and wrestle with Lily. He had tossed his glove and Lily had dropped to the grass rolling over onto her back so he could rub her belly. He giggled and tumbled on top of her as she rolled out from under him. Pinning him to the green grass, she licked his face. He laughed hysterically while trying to squirm out from under her huge paws.

As I watched with joy the laughter started to fade. I tilted my head as it began to sound hollow and tinny. Things started to get dark and fuzzy. I heard myself saying no over and over again as the whole scene went dark. Confused, I tried reach out for Justin and felt that my hands were wet. Where was Justin? Justin? What the fuck? Justin was gone, taken from me long ago. I felt the empty hole in the pit of my stomach open again and I missed him so very much at that moment.

I was cold, very cold, and wet. I opened my eyes slightly and saw that I was laying face down on the slush covered ground. I wiped the tears away with the back of my dirty hands and groaned as I moved. Every inch of my body hurt and I began to push myself up out of the semi frozen slush. Stars exploded in front of my eyes as something hit me hard in the back of my skull. I moaned just before my head hit the ground.

"Stay the fuck down asshole," I heard come from behind me.

I blinked a few times to try and clear my vision. I shook my head to do the same to my mind. What happened? How the fuck did I get here?

"Get this prick in the truck, pronto," I heard seconds before someone grabbed me under my arms and hoisted me up.

I saw olive drab out of the corner of my eye and instantly knew I was in a world of shit. Oh yeah, I remember now what happened. Oh, this was truly gonna suck.

Two soldiers dragged me through the slush and another two grabbed me under the arms. They quickly pulled me up into the back of a two and a half ton truck. They shoved me down onto the bench seat on the right side.

"Sit there and don't make a fucking sound," one of them said as he cuffed my hands in front of me.

"Understand?" he asked as he grabbed me by the throat and started to squeeze my wind pipe shut.

I nodded slowly and hung my head after he let go. I heard others get in and the truck start up. Someone gave the all clear and the truck began to roll. I stared down at my cuffed wrists and went over how I had gotten here step by step…

It had been a week or so since the incident at the boys club and everyone was home safe. Things had gotten back to a semblance of normalcy. Drake and Sam had announced that they were pregnant and everyone seemed particularly happy. We had also found a steady supply of fuel that didn't require us stealing it from the government. As bad as the world was in general, things seemed as if they were on an upswing.

It was dark and I was in bed curled up with Chris under our sleeping bags. I heard Lily stir and growl low in her throat seconds before I heard someone calling my name from out in the kitchen. Lily barked once and I rolled quickly out of bed and pulled open the door before whoever it was woke everyone else in the house. Dan, a patrol leader who helped out in the comm. center, stood there in the nearly pitch black kitchen. All I could clearly see was the white's of his eyes which were wide open in almost panic.

"What's up? What time is it?" I whispered as I leaned close to him.

"It's two thirty in the morning and they're comin' Mack, like now," He whispered back desperately.

"FUCK! Go now, wake everyone else down here!" I barked as I dove back inside to get Chris.

"Honey, what's wrong?" she mumbled.

"Get up. We gotta go, right now, UP!" I said trying to keep panic out of my voice as I pulled up my black cargo pants and grabbed my Sig out of the drawer next to the bed.

Chris sat bolt up and gasped as she realized what I was saying. She was up, had pants on and was pulling a heavy sweater over her head by the time I had slapped on my boots. She grabbed her gun out of the drawer next to her side of the bed and checked the safety before stuffing it into the small of her back.

"Get Lily out onto the porch, I'll be right back," I said as I bolted out through the kitchen and onto the porch.

I grabbed the knob on the old door that led to the second floor and shoved my way through it, calling up the stairs as I took them two at a time. With the little light coming in through the window I could see Liam was standing in the kitchen with his "multi-tasker" when I rounded the top of the stairs. It was his stripped down AR-15 with a collapsible stock, a shotgun attachment slung under the barrel and a variable zoom scope on top. Liam was a big fan of fucking things up near or far.

"We gotta go, now, they're coming and I have no idea how close they are," I said breathing a little heavy.

"We'll be down in less than two minutes," he said calmly as he turned and went back into his and Anne's bedroom.

I could hear that she was already up and getting ready to move by the time I headed back down the stairs. When I got to the porch again Chris, Lily and Dan were out there waiting for me. In under a minute Tom and AJ had joined us. They had taken the other two bedrooms on the first floor and were busy tying up their boots and tossing on jackets as we waited for Anne and Liam to join us. Anne came down carrying her chrome .357. It wasn't the only gun she had, just her favorite. I finished tying my boot as well, stood up and took a quick head count to make sure we had everyone before I headed out into the yard toward the hole in the fence that led us to the back door of the shop.

I made my way quickly through the fence and jogged down toward the door that led us inside. Liam was bringing up the rear while Lily ran in tight circles around us herding us toward the shop. We moved almost silently and as much as I strained I couldn't hear any vehicles in the dead of the night. Hopefully, that gave us at least ten minutes. I yanked open the door and was nearly blinded by the electric light that was glaring inside. I shooed everyone inside and hurried down the old wooden stairs where George stood in his comm. center packing up his equipment as fast as his chubby little hands would let him.

"It's about time you fuckin' got here," he said almost panting as he handed me an ear bud and a radio so we could all stay in contact.

"How long?" I asked as I watched him hand out the same to everyone who had shown up.

"Not nearly fuckin' long enough, we may have fifteen at the very most. They were at the town line when I sent for you," He answered shoving more of his equipment into an old comic book box.

"Lovely," I said rolling my eyes.

Drake came jogging up to our little gaggle with his black shirt unbuttoned, boots untied and trying to get his hair pulled back out of his face.

"They comin'?" he asked as he finished with his hair.

"Yep," I answered with a nod.

"Fuck," was his only comment.

"Okay, George, Gomez, AJ and Tom stay here. Drake, find Teddy and get everyone else up to the armory now," I said trying to work something out in my head and still keep everyone alive.

"George what're they comin' with?" I asked.

"Cain's guy says he saw one Humvee two 2 ½ tons and a jeep so I'd have to guess no more than thirty," he said as he grabbed something off his desk and handed it to me with a knowing nod.

"Yeah, no way that's a supply convoy," I said more to myself than anyone else as I returned the nod and knelt down. I untied my left boot. I slid it off and placed the small round piece of black plastic in under the cushion and put my boot back on.

"How many people are here right now?" I asked as I finished retying it.

"With all of you, maybe twenty-five," Gomez answered.

"Okay, Gomez you take your team and make sure George gets mobile. Run dark and stay away from this area. Avoid the main roads," I said as I turned to leave the comm. center.

"Got it boss," he said.

"We gonna use the old backup spot Mack?" George asked as he shoved his revolver in to its holster.

"Yeah, the old hospital on the hill will be our new home for a bit. Don't go until after dawn and make sure you don't leave any obvious tracks," I said from the doorway.

"I know it's been awhile but I do still remember how to be sneaky," he said sounding indignant.

"We'll be up as soon as we can," I said with a wink.

"Be careful," George said.

"Always," I replied, "Stay safe Gomez. AJ, Tom with me," I said as I left the comm. center doorway and ran down the long hallway that led down to my office.

"What was that thing George handed you?" AJ asked jogging behind me.

"Just something we may need if this doesn't work out is all," was all I gave him as a response.

We had known that the army was going to be showing up eventually. I was pretty sure they had gotten all the intel that the captain had gathered from Mikey when they kidnapped him a few weeks ago. The problem was that we had no way of knowing if that information had been passed on to army HQ in Boston. So until now we had been waiting to see if the other shoe dropped. Now, we had proof that they did indeed know where the shop was and from the papers we collected from the boy's club, they knew where all our safe houses and storage areas were as well.

George and I had been working quietly over the last week to move what supplies we could and tried to figure out where to move our shop to just in case they did get a hold of everything. We decided on what had been my original idea for our base of operations. It had been an old abandoned hospital that sat at the very top of a steep hill off one the main roads of town. It was nearly perfect. Easily defensible, well away from any main road, it had its own generators and had one small street that led to it with a tiny dirt road that could be used in emergencies. We had originally shelved the idea because it was too out of the way. We wanted to be near some of the other people in town so they knew where to find us if they needed help.

We got down to my office and after AJ and Tom got inside I closed the door behind us. I walked over to my desk and grabbed my AK-47 from behind it. I tossed my shotgun to AJ and followed that with a bandolier of shells. I slid into my harness and put the two pistols in their cross draw holsters. I picked the AK up off the desk and leaned against the front of it.

"I need to talk to you both for a minute before we catch up with everyone else," I said cryptically.

"What's up boss?" AJ asked as he loaded the shotgun.

"In a little bit I may give you both a specific order, don't ask, you'll know it when you hear it. I need you both to promise me that you'll follow that order without question or hesitation. I need to know now that you can do this because if I'm right it will be a split second timing thing," I said looking at them both.

"Yeah, we can do that… I think. You're not gonna order us to shoot you right?" Tom asked with a smile.

"No, dear God no, I promise I won't ask you to do that," I said shaking my head.

"Well sure, in that case we can definitely do it," AJ said.

"You're not gonna tell us what it is though are you?" Tom asked.

"No, what it is isn't important. I just need you both to trust me. I'm hoping that if all goes well I won't even have to worry about it, but I need to know you'll both do what I ask if I **do** need to," I said heading toward them and the door.

"We will," Tom said.

"I promise," AJ added.

"Good, and thank you. Let's get up to the armory," I said as I opened the door and turned off the light.

Chapter 2

Everyone we had was in the armory by the time AJ, Tom and I arrived. Gomez, his team and George had left. They would try and maintain radio contact as long as they were able to. Luke and Drake were hurriedly handing out weapons and ammo to everyone. Teddy was with Anne, Chris, Sam and Liam trying to get caught up on what was going on while he finished getting dressed. I walked over toward them and motioned for Teddy as AJ and Tom grabbed some extra ammo and weapons.

"What's up Mack?" Teddy asked as he jogged over to me.

"Need to talk to you for a sec is all," I said as we stepped away from everyone.

"I need you and your team to get Liam and the girls out safely," I said.

"I figured they'd go with you and Alpha team," he said sounding confused.

"No, I'd feel safer if she was with you and your team. We're gonna be tied up here and I need someone I trust to get them out," I said as I gave his shoulder a squeeze to emphasize the point.

"Yeah, of course Mack, anything you need me to do," he said suddenly very serious.

"Good," I said with a nod.

"Take them out the bulkhead on the west side and grab one of the vehicles in the lot behind the church," I said speaking quicker now.

"Where we goin' once I have a car?" Teddy asked.

"We're gonna set up at the old hospital on the hill. Don't get too close until around dawn. Make sure everything has died down before you even get close though," I said as I made my way back to the counter.

"Got it Mack," he said with a nod.

"Just please make sure they're safe no matter what," I said as I grabbed as many extra clips as I could hold.

"Of course I will Mack, they're family. Besides, you're not gonna be far behind us right?" he asked.

"Yeah, of course, Alpha will be right behind you," I said with a smile plastered on my face.

"That's what I like to hear. A good strong positive attitude in the face of certain death," he said as he laughed and went to gather up his team.

I made my way over to Chris and the others. I knelt down and scruffled the fur on Lily's neck. I gave her a kiss on the head. I looked up and saw the four of them staring down waiting for me to update them. I chuckled softly and stood. Liam had grabbed a couple other back up pieces and a small bag full of extra clips. I gotta give the man credit he did like to be prepared.

"You guys are gonna go with Teddy. He's gonna make sure you're taken care of and get to the new shop safely," I said as I gave Anne and Sam a quick hug.

"Wouldn't it be better if we stayed with you?" Chris asked as she gave me a dirty look.

"No it wouldn't actually. Teddy is leaving as soon as his team is geared up. Me, Drake and the rest of us are gonna be a bit behind you all. It's our job to stay here and hold them off so they don't just chase us all down. Your job is to get safe and make sure our wounded stay alive honey," I said calmly.

"Promise me you'll be careful," she said.

"I promise. I'll be along as soon as I can," I said as I leaned down, kissed her lips softly and then again on her forehead.

"I love you angel," I said softly as I cupped her face and stared into her eyes.

"I love you too," she said not breaking our gaze.

"Good, go with Teddy then and make sure everyone is safe. They know where the clinic is. Hopefully, Lou will meet us there with as many supplies as he can get out," I said as I nodded to Teddy.

"We're all ready to go Mack," Teddy said as he came over.

"Good, remember out the west bulkhead," I said as I grabbed my AK off the counter.

"Yep, got it Mack, stay safe bro we'll see you in a bit," Teddy said as he nodded. His team led Chris and the others out the door and down the stairs.

I watched them go and gave a heavy sigh as I headed to the door. The armory was mostly empty now. Everyone had grabbed their weapons and ammo before heading to the staging area. Drake came up beside me and we both made our way down the hall toward the east side. There was a flurry of men around us. The whole place was emotionally charged and ready to blow. We may not be the best soldiers around but every one of the men left in the shop knew that if we didn't hold them off long enough that no one was gonna be safe.

"We are clear Baby Bear," I heard George say through my earpiece.

"Copy that. Ratchet is on her way as well," I answered.

Ratchet was short for nurse Ratchet, which was our call sign for Chris. I wanted George to know that she was safely on her way and that he should be keeping an eye out for her when he gets to the new shop. I tried to put thoughts of her out of my head. I knew she'd be safe with Teddy and Liam with her. Plus, she had Lily and to be honest Chris was pretty tough as well when she needed to be. I wasn't gonna do anyone any good worrying about her, when I should be worried about my own ass.

I got down to the comm. center and headed into the kitchen. Two of our teams were there, the room had three entrances. Two were on direct routes from different doors to get into the shop. The third door led to the living quarters across the hallway. We had a third team set up on the other end on the building in case they found their way into one of the far side doors. The boys flipped up a few tables on their sides for cover and were now in position waiting for the army to breach.

"I heard motors when we came by the comm. center, shouldn't be more than a minute or two," Drake said, as he knelt behind one of the tables.

"Okay boys, let's stay…" was all I got to say before I heard the heavy door at the top of the stairs blow off its' hinges.

I heard Chris scream in my earpiece at the explosion.

"Frosty," I said under my breath as I tensed up.

There was a hollow "**thunk, thunk, thunk**," as a canister rolled down to the bottom of the stairs. Tom yelled "smoke" a second before I heard the dull "**Thud**" of it detonating. A bright green plume of smoke filled the comm. center and billowed toward us. We had left the door to the

20

kitchen open so we had a good line of fire when they got to the bottom of the stairs. That was all a pipe dream now. I saw movement in the smoke and opened up with a short burst, it stopped moving quickly.

More men hit the bottom of the stairs now firing into the kitchen before they even got to the bottom step. We dropped behind the cover of the tables and fired around the edges. I heard the other team yell over the gunfire that they had movement from the other door. I saw blue smoke mingling with the green as I chanced a peek in their direction. AJ stood behind his table and opened up with the shotgun, unloading all seven rounds as fast as he could pump. They returned fire and shards of his table went flying as he ducked back to reload. I heard the rattle of M-16's off to my right and knew that the army was close to the door now on the other side of the room. The other team returned fire and held them off for a short while. I heard a grunt and saw that we had lost one already.

"I think it's almost time to go," Drake said as he scooted over toward me.

I nodded, popped up and sprayed the doorway. I heard at least one go down but there were more of them pushing him forward even as he fell. I called for both teams to fall back. The other team left the safety of their tables and headed for the far doorway that led to a corridor. We covered them as best we could but they took heavy fire and someone caught one in the shoulder before they could get to safety.

I heard Billy, the other squad leader, give me a three count and we started to move as they laid down cover fire for us. We got lucky and made it around the corner without any problems. Our team sprayed down the room as best we could while Billy's team reloaded.

"TEDDY ARE YOU CLEAR?" I called into my mic.

21

"Can't talk now Mack, lil busy," was what I got in return. I could hear small arms fire coming from somewhere around him.

"Mack, they just breached our door as well, taking pretty heavy fire," I heard Roy report over the din from the third teams' position.

"Billy, get your team and head out toward Roy. Clear that squad and then get out that door. Take Roy's team with you. You know what to do after that," I yelled into Billy's ear as I leaned in close to him.

"Sir, you gonna be okay here?" he asked.

"Yeah were gonna cover your exit and then we're gonna try to get out through the bulkhead like Teddy's doing," I answered.

He gave a nod and tapped his men on the shoulders as they returned fire into the kitchen. One by one they emptied their rifles, got up and headed down the hallway behind their team leader. AJ, Tom and Drake had taken their positions in the doorway and I stood behind AJ who had knelt on the left side of the door. I squeezed off a few rounds and changed out my clip.

"Mack we're outside and clear for the moment," I heard Teddy say in my earpiece.

"Copy that, Alpha is heading that way momentarily. Get as far away as you can Teddy, don't stick around," I said as Drake gave me a nod and got ready for us to move.

"Copy that," I heard Teddy answer.

"Drake's on point, head to the west bulkhead door," I said as Drake slid past me, I brought up the rear laying down rounds around the doorway as I backed down the corridor.

We made it to the end of the hall before we heard the army get to the doorway we were just in. We picked up the pace and hurried down the hall toward the west side of the building. Rounds zipped over our heads and I heard the short bursts behind me as we got to a T intersection in the hall. I dove to my left into the adjoining hallway with Tom while AJ and Drake dove right into a supply closet. Drake was up first firing away. Tom crawled forward a few feet and opened up with a couple of short bursts. It pinned their heads down for a few seconds but we had to clear them out before we could move again. Before I had time to take two seconds to think of what to do more rounds snapped over my head from behind this time.

"SHIT THEY'RE BEHIND US!" I yelled as I spun and let loose in a wild spray.

"MOVE, MOVE, MOVE!" I said as I yanked Tom to his feet and shoved him in front of me before they returned fire.

Tom stumbled out into the hall in front of me and fell again as he twisted to fire down at the other squad. I grabbed him by his shirt and pulled him out of the intersection while he emptied his clip at them to keep them buttoned up tight. I felt hands on my shoulders and heard Drake yelling for me to get into the room across the hall from where he and AJ had been. It was the lower floor of our little library, mostly empty except for a couple counters. There were some folding chairs over in the corner and some half filled book cases.

The four of us tumbled into the room. AJ slammed the door shut and locked it as we all gasped for air. I was up first checking the room to see if it was clear and to make sure we hadn't trapped ourselves in here with no other exits. Within a couple seconds I remembered there were two other doors, one led in the direction we needed to go and unfortunately one led to the hall with one of the army squads in it. Drake realized it shortly after I did and bolted over to lock it.

"Mack, we're clear and we have transport, just waitin'" on you guys," I heard Teddy say into my earpiece.

"What the fuck? That was not the plan. Get them the fuck out of here!" I said to Teddy as I moved behind one of the counters. There's no way we had more than a minute or so before they blew through those doors.

"I tried that already Mack. Ratchet refuses to leave without you," Teddy said, sounding annoyed.

"She's a hundred and ten pounds soaking wet asshole! **PUT** her in the car and go! That is not a request!" I growled.

The thin plywood door was suddenly riddled with holes as bullets quickly tore through it. AJ and Tom stood behind their counter and tried to hold them off.
"YOU ARE NOT LEAVING WITHOUT MY FUCKING HUSBAND!" I heard Chris scream in my earpiece.

I heard a grunt and Drake glanced at me curiously as he heard it too. The second door flew open as one of the army guys kicked it in. Rounds flew from both sides. I heard Drake yelp behind me.

"I do **NOT** have fucking time for this! Get her secured Ted!" I yelled between bursts.

"She fucking hit me!" Teddy whined.

"Deal with it," I think I heard Roy say. "We are all clear here, they broke off and ran. We are going to sneak our way to our new home on foot. Stay safe and see you soon."

"Copy that," I said as I sat on the floor and leaned back against the counter to change out my clip.

Drake had taken one in the shoulder. He said it was a scratch but I wasn't sure. I took a second to glance over at the other counter. AJ and Tom seemed okay, so I figured it was time for us to move again. Then, I heard another "**thunk**" as something landed in the room on the other side of the counter. Tom popped up to open fire and I heard him curse before the pop of whatever it was. The room lit up and there was a huge bang as Tom screamed and fell backwards.

"**Flashbang!**" AJ yelled.

Before we could even react they were almost on top of us. Drake burst out from behind the counter and emptied his clip into the doorway in front of him. I dropped my AK and pulled both pistols as I stood. I got cracked in the jaw and I wheeled back, firing blindly in front of me. I heard him grunt and fall as I spun to meet another one who was coming up behind me. I swung with my left and clocked him hard in the side of the head with the butt of the Sig. As he stumbled back I shot him twice in the chest. There was small arms fire all around me. Drake had pulled his pistol and was beating one guy with it next to the doorway. AJ had another one by the back of his helmet and was unloading into his gut. Tom was on the ground rolling with one soldier. He was on his back trying to free his gun hand that the soldier had held to the floor. The soldier had lost his helmet in the fray and I put one in the top of his head as I strode toward them.

More of them poured through the doors and Drake had one pinned to the wall by his throat. He didn't see the one coming behind him, aiming the butt of his rifle at the back of his head. I dove between them and caught the rifle on the down swing with my forearm. Pain shot all the way up to my shoulder. I used my free hand to grab him by the harness and shoved him back toward the counter. He made a grunting sound as his back slammed against the old wooden counter and pushed all the air out of his lungs. I pulled him forward and spun him around as I hooked my sore left arm up under his shoulder. I snaked my hand around the back of his neck and slid my right hand up under his chin. With a severe jerking motion I pulled his chin in one direction and shoved his head in the other. I heard a sickening crack and he went limp in my arms. AJ slammed into me almost full speed as I let the body drop.

"We gotta go there's too many," he said as one long word as he spun me around and pushed me toward the only clear door out of the room.

"GOGOGO!" Drake yelled from behind me.

I pulled my pistols as AJ forced me through the doorway and into a seemingly empty hall. Drake was behind him. He had grabbed a dropped M-16 and darted ahead of me to make sure we were clear. Tom brought up the rear. He had grabbed my AK and hosed down the room with rounds to give us a couple seconds. I tossed him one of my spare clips as we moved down the side hall and back into the main. We made it to the end of the hall and hooked a left. The side hall had a door on the right hand side that led into the old theater at the end of our block. Since we were on the basement level we ended up in what used to be the old storage area. Over in the corner was a rickety set of wooden stairs that ended at the bulkhead doors I told Teddy to go out. They opened up onto Medford Street which ran alongside the shop.

Once we got inside we closed and locked the door. It was almost pitch black in here but we all knew where the door was. We had left it for storage but there wasn't a lot left in here. The flimsy door wasn't gonna hold them long so I knew I had to work quickly. We moved quietly across the dark room and set up in front of the stairs. I signaled a halt and called for Teddy.

"Yeah boss," He answered.

"Are you still stupidly outside?" I asked angrily.

"I just finally got her in the car," he said apologetically.

"Fine, hold one," I said as I turned to Tom.

"Grab him and get the hell out of here…now," I ordered as I nodded toward Drake.

"What the fuck?" Drake said looking confused.

"Now AJ!" I yelled.

To AJ's credit he didn't question me at all. He turned and scooped up Drake. He tossed him over his broad shoulder and headed toward the stairs. Tom followed him and kept glancing back at me with a completely baffled look on his face.

"I don't have time to explain, just help AJ get him outside and in that car, now," I said as I turned and walked away from the stairwell.

"Teddy, package is coming out now. Open the doors, and then get the fuck out of here pronto," I said just before I heard the first kick on the door.

"What the fuck are you doing? Lemme GO! **I WILL FUCKING KILL YOU!**" I heard Drake screaming as AJ got to the top of the stairs.

The bulkhead doors flung open and Teddy grabbed the back of Drakes shirt. He pulled him out with AJ and Tom closed the doors after taking a second to spare a last worried look.

"MACK, I KNOW YOU CAN FUCKING HEAR ME YOU FUCK! GET OUT HERE NOW!" Drake screamed in my earpiece.

"Teddy, go. Please just trust me and go. They're coming," I said quietly as they kicked again at the door.

"We're leaving now Mack. I don't like it but we're going. Stay safe bro," Teddy said sounding beaten. I could hear Chris crying and Drake swearing in the background.

Then I was alone… until they finished kicking in the door.

Chapter 3

This seemed like such a good idea when I came up with it. I mean hell it was me they wanted, so why not give me to them. Now I was scared shitless. I tried to focus while dropped the clips out of my pistols and slapped fresh ones home. My heart was pounding in my chest. I took a deep breath and tried to stem the panic from rising. Pulling my ear bud out, I dropped it into my breast pocket. the mic was still on so they could hear me but I really didn't need any distractions right now.

I know that neither Drake nor Chris would believe me but it was never my intention to get captured. The plan was for them to chase me around in here for a bit, while I thinned the herd and everyone else got far away. Then I could hopefully make my way to a different exit and slip quietly into the night while they were stuck here cleaning up. At this point though, I'm just hoping to see my friends and family again. I heard two quick kicks then the flimsy door flew open, bounced off the wall and swung slowly back at an odd angle. I closed my eyes and took a breath, listening to them rush into the room.

I gritted my teeth and took a step sideways as I scanned the room quickly for targets. There were at least five visible and I started from right to left. I fired off two rounds and watched as only one found its mark. He spun but didn't go down. The next two landed dead center of mass and the soldier next to him dropped like a stone as I took another two steps to my left. I was heading for the stairs that led up to the first floor. After that it gets a bit blurry. They opened up with their M-16's and I rattled off rounds, bolting for the stairs. I glanced over my shoulder and saw that their numbers had at least been whittled down by half.

Slugs pounded into the landing as I made it to the top of the long stairway. Grabbing an empty rolling mini-bar that had been left in the corner I shoved it, sending it tumbling down toward them. I was sure it wouldn't do much but I didn't need it to. It just needed to buy me a couple seconds to get down the hall and around a corner so I wasn't such a sitting duck. I turned and ran smack dab into a young kid barreling toward me. His look of surprise quickly turned to fear as he watched me empty my pistols into his chest. He continued forward a step or two before thudding face first into the plush theater carpeting. He didn't move again. I dropped my empty guns and grabbed his rifle. I bolted down the hall and prayed to get behind cover before they reached the top of the stairs.

I hooked another right and ran down the hall. I felt too expsoed and ducked into what used to be an old convenience store. Now it was basically a wide open and thankfully empty space. I ran across it full tilt to the door on the other side and listened at it. Not hearing anything right off the bat I opened it and slid through closing it quietly behind me. Another few rooms and I could get access to the roof. From there I could sneak around and find a safe way down. I quickly moved across and into the next room over which was the armory. Checking this door as well and after a second or two popping it open and ducked inside.

I gasped a quick breath as I heard, "Gotcha you fuck!"

A hand slid up over my mouth and another tried to wrap around my shoulders. I started to pull forward and saw the other one that was now in front of me, smiling, as he went to raise his rifle. I swung the butt of my gun upwards and connected with the bottom of his jaw. He fell back hard. Little prick won't be fucking smiling anytime soon. Biting the hand that was over my mouth, I heard a muffled curse and tasted blood as his hand fell away. I spun, dropped my weapon and in one motion threw myself at the guy behind me as he tried to pull his pistol. I slammed his hand off the ground a few times until he dropped it and punched him in the face. Rage and fear coursed through me as I beat him harder and harder. His jaw broke and it just made me hit him more. He was out for good and the second guy had recovered. I heard him behind me a split second too late. He grabbed me and tried to pull me off his buddy. I reached back and got him by the scruff of the neck. Using him as leverage I shoved myself to my feet, throwing us both backwards as hard as I could. It was enough to throw off his balance and we tumbled to the ground. I landed on top of him and drove my elbow hard into his ribcage. There was a "**woof**" as I drove the breath out of him. I rolled to my right and popped up. Kicking him in the face and roaring as I yanked him off the floor by his combat harness. I smashed the back of his head off the wall and hit him with a solid right cross.

"STAY THE FUCK OUT OF MY HOUSE!" I screamed as pummeling his face until it was practically unrecognizable.

I finally realized that he was at least out cold and took a panicked look around to make sure I was still alone. The body slid to the floor as I bent forward and put my hands on my knees. I was gasping for breath and the adrenaline was flowing full out. After a few seconds I grabbed a rifle and stumbled over to the door leading into the hallway. I calmed myself, but only barely, my hands were shaking and I was starting to tremble. I got stupid and flung open the door without checking it. At the top of the stairs leading down was another patrol. The guy in front made a surprised sound and I kicked him solidly in the chest sending him flying back into the other two behind him. They all crashed to the bottom and I ran to my right making my way to the kitchen in the old Chinese restaurant. I closed the door quickly and worked my way toward the front. I found the stairs that led me back down into the basement. Change of plans, if I could make it down and across just a little bit further I could pop out one of the small vent windows that led to the street.

I hit the bottom of the stairs and listened at the corner for a moment. Thinking it was clear I swung myself around the corner. There was a feeling of abject terror as I saw this massive hand wrap around the barrel of my M-16. As it shoved the barrel toward the ceiling I pulled the trigger and fired blindly as the other hand pounded me just in front of my left temple. A quick glimpse was all I caught of the behemoth in front of me as my left eye started to swell shut. He nailed me again in the same spot as he twisted the rifle, pulled it out of my hands and tossed it behind him. I tried to gather myself but he connected again, with the side of my skull this time, sending stars shooting across my field of vision. I stumbled, he grabbed me by the throat and pinned me against the wall. I kicked hard at his gut and got a smile in return. He squeezed tighter as I reached down and pulled my blade out of the sheath in my boot. I flipped it around and drove it straight up into his arm. He grunted but his grip held. I was starting to black out, the edges of my vision were beginning to go dark. I brought the blade up and tried not to close my eyes as I drove it down into the back of his meaty hand. It bit into my flesh and dinged off of my collarbone. It hurt like hell but it worked. He screamed and dropped me.

He stumbled back and pulled the knife out of his hand while glaring at me and roaring. Leaning against the wall coughing and choking I tried to suck in as much air as possible. He charged at me and I dove to my left as he barreled into the wall where I had just been. Yanking out my other boot knife, I pushed myself up. My legs felt like rubber. He spun and charged me again with a growl from deep in his throat. Flipping the knife in my hand so the blade was flush against my forearm, I slashed him across the cheek and sidestepped as he dove at me. He was all brute strength, no finesse. He was in a rage and the blood was freely flowing down the side of his face as he grabbed at me.

I felt his fingers graze against my ribs as he went by. I stuck my left hand out and caught the back of his collar. I pulled back, trying to rear him like a horse while stuffing my blade deep into his kidney. He howled and thrashed and slammed me again with that beefy paw of his swatting me like a fly. He flailed at the wound on his back as I pressed the attack. I caught him up under his ribs. He stopped howling and stared blankly down at me. I put my hand on his shoulder and shoved the blade deeper and he gasped.

He leaned forward onto me, his hands still reaching for my throat. I could feel his ragged breath on my face, I jerked the blade again. He had slouched down so far now that we were eye to eye. He stumbled forward a few steps driving me backwards down the hall. He was gurgling as he took a breath and I could see the fear on his face. Blood began to run out of his mouth and he gasped one last breath before his head hit my shoulder. I felt him tremble a few times before he went still.

The body dropped as I leaned against the wall. I gasped and choked while trying to catch my breath, just praying to not throw up. Still winded and shaking I stumbled down the hall, ducking around a corner trying to find my way out. I saw the small rectangular window a couple yards down the hall and made my way toward it. Strangely, it was silent as I limped down to the window. I could hear my breathing and as the adrenaline started to wane, began to feel the pain in my legs, chest, collarbone, neck, and most especially my head. I undid the latch and groaned as I shoved it open a couple inches. Using the last of my strength to pull myself up and wedge my shoulders through the frame. I planted my hands into the soggy snow covered ground. Wiggling the rest of the way through and out to freedom. Smiling, I pushed myself off the wet ground a second before I heard someone yell "Take him!" and then everything went black.

Chapter 4

"This piece of shit better be worth it Sampson. More than half of my squad is dead or wounded." Someone said across from me, bringing me out of my reverie.

"I know man, I know. He is the last of them though Hughes. At least we'll get some down time to heal up after this," I heard someone I'm assuming was Sampson, answer.

I raised my head and glanced over at Sampson who was sitting across from me. He had dark brown or black hair that was a little longer than it probably should have been, a heavy five o'clock shadow and a squared off jaw. His uniform was dirty and he was sportin' sergeant stripes. I glanced to my right at Hughes and saw that he had the same stripes on his arm but the similarities ended there. He had a much rounder face that was clean shaven, high and tight, light brown hair and his uniform seemed almost freshly pressed. Obviously, Sergeant Hughes had stayed outside the shop for today's visit.

Hughes caught me checking him out, raised an eyebrow momentarily and then looked away dismissively with a low grunt. There were others in the back of the truck with us. Most were just quietly riding along though. They were tired and worn down. Hughes had made it sound like they had been on the move a lot lately. Maybe, they were just silently waiting to get home alive.

We were coming through Harvard square now on our ride eastward. From what I could see out of the open flap on the back of the truck it looked almost the same as it always had, just with infinitely less people now. I watched quietly as we made our way past the old, long deserted buildings of Harvard University with its' ivy covered buildings. They no longer had the lush green plants growing all up their esteemed red brick walls. What they did have was the remnants of the withered vines clinging to the cracked brick looking like dried veins.

"Hope you said your goodbye's pally, chances are you won't be seein' home anytime soon, if ever." Sampson said.

"Ya think so huh?" I asked as I glanced up at him with a small smile.

"Oh, you can think your gonna worm your way out all you want but from what I hear, you ain't goin anywhere. You've been way too much trouble for command," he replied.

"Yeah, commands gonna make you cry for your momma and break you but good," interjected Hughes.

"As much as I hate agreeing with cornbread over there, he is right. They're gonna fuck your shit up." Sampson agreed.

"We'll see," I said with a nod.

I pretended to know what I was doing. Truth is I had no idea at all and that scared the shit out of me. I had never met command or even been to the Boston command center so I had no idea what I was dealing with. I've never been a fan of charging blindly into a situation but I didn't see any other way this time. I sat there hoping I hadn't just made a seriously bad call.

"We'll see he says," Hughes said mockingly.

"What the hell is wrong with you folk up here that you can't ever just do what you're told? You ain't goin nowhere no time soon son, accept that. Deal with it and you'll be much better off," Hughes said.

"Well hayseed, the difference up here is that we like to think for ourselves instead of just following along blindly like the sheep that you all used to raise out there. I am assuming from your accent and attitude that you are from somewhere in the Midwest," I said as I leaned back against the side of the truck and closed my one good eye for a minute to try and gather a thought or two.

"Where I'm from ain't none yer damn business you thievin' fuck. It's called following orders and it's what a good soldier does!" Hughes yelled.

"I have never once been a soldier, much less a good one," I said with a shrug. Pleased I'd managed to piss him off.

Sampson smiled and shook his head, "He's baitin' you cornbread. He's tryin' to get you to do something stupid so he can use it to his advantage."

"I knew that jackhole!" Hughes bellowed, turning a lovely shade of red.

"Uh huh." Sampson said rolling his eyes.

"You're just as bad as these thievin' scumbags some days Sampson. You and the rest of your New York buddies act like you know everything as well. I swear it must be something in the water up here makes all you assholes think you're all so much better than the rest of us," Hughes said before he whipped his helmet into the far corner of the truck to vent his obvious frustrations.

"Or we just are," both Sampson and I said at almost the very same instant under our breaths.

We glanced at each other and I could swear I saw a small smile cross his face. I sat back and squared my shoulders. He saw my move and remained hunched forward. I raised an eyebrow and tilted my head at him questioningly. I mouthed the word "why" at him and he cocked his head at me.

"Why are you even with them?" I asked quietly as I leaned forward to somewhat hide my face in shadow. I hoped I could be heard over the rumbling of the truck.

"They make sure my family is fed, warm and safe," he said with a shrug. "Why are you not?"

"We've been fine without them so far. I don't want them telling us what to do. They don't even know us and they did a crappy job of it before the storm," I said trying to be succinct.

"You sure that's all?" he asked.

"What else would it be?" I asked accusingly.

"You sure you just don't wanna give up all that power?" he asked.

"Power? I don't have any power. I work my ass off to keep my people alive that's all," I said getting a little loud.

"Don't you though? You are in charge of your clan," he said.

"I am, and they **ASKED** me to be. I didn't demand it of them. The big difference is that I am right there with them. Not a thousand miles away living the easy life while they suffer while still claiming that I represent their interests. I know them… **ALL** of them, and I would do anything to protect them," I said defiantly.

"Including letting yourself be caught?" he said, with a smirk.

"Dunno what the fuck you're talkin' about," I said, trying to not look shocked.

"Yeah, I'm sure you don't," he said, with a nod.

We fell silent and I sat there staring at my boots. We both were doing what we had to do to protect our families. Each way made sense and neither was the easy path. Unfortunately, we weren't gonna agree anytime soon it seemed.

A short time later the truck shifted gears and started to slow down. I tried to catch a peek out of the back and couldn't really see much out the back of the truck. I knew we had gone over the bridge and into Boston proper. We had just gone over the Charles River a couple minutes ago, so we weren't too deep in town yet. Sampson saw my curiosity and chuckled.

"You'll know as soon as we go through the gates. It's hard not to. God I always hated this place," he said smiling.

"No fuckin' way," was the thought that went through my head. There's only one place in Boston a true New Yorker hates. They made their base of operations Fenway Park?

The truck came to a stop. I heard voices yelling back and forth. It roared and lurched forward rolling slowly. I started to see electric light coming around the edges of the back of the truck. I gazed out the back as we passed through the gates and blinked trying to adjust to the brightness now filling the covered bed. I could see the large green doors swinging shut behind us as we made our way right onto what used to be the infield of Fenway Park. I made a choking sound as we came to a stop near what should be second base.

They had erected their barracks and Quonset huts all over the field in a very organized manner. They were using the old lights to make it bright as day here and very easy to see anyone trying to sneak in or out. I'm not sure how they were running the electricity but they seemed to have plenty of it.

"Alright let's go." Sampson said, as he said and grabbed me by the arm, leading me to the back of the truck bed.

"I'll take him Sampson!" Hughes yelled, jumping up from the bench seat.

"I got it cornbread." Sampson said, as I made my way down out of the back of the truck, which was not all that easy with my hands cuffed.

"Holy shit," Was all I could manage to get out as I gazed around at how they had taken something that was once so dear to us and turned it in to something barely recognizable.

I mean, I guess it made sense in a strange way. It had huge walls around it like a castle, lots of places to station men around the top so they had a very defensible position. It was also a wide enough open space so they had room to house all the troops as well as facilities to support them all. It is also located near the river so they could easily send and receive supplies and more men if necessary. All in all, it was actually a pretty damn good idea, even though I hated the very thought of it.

"Alright, you've had enough of a look around, let's go." Sampson said with a nudge.

"Bet they didn't do this to Yankee stadium huh?" I asked.

"Nahh, they set up in grand central down there." Sampson answered as we walked toward the bullpen in right field.

"Hmm musta just been that Yankee stadium wasn't good enough for them to use," I said hoping for a laugh.

"Yeah smartass that's it," he said. I could hear the smile though.

We walked through a guarded door and under what used to be the right field bleachers. We entered a wide hallway and turned right. After we had walked a dozen yards or so we came to a door. Sampson opened the door and let me through into a stairwell.

"Down ya go," he said, again behind me.

I made my way down the stairs to the bottom and another door. He opened this one as well and told me to "Go right," I did as I was told. We may have had a couple things in common but I was still cuffed and could only see out of one eye. I wasn't about to piss this guy off and maybe get beat some more if not killed. We walked down the wide concrete hall for awhile and finally came to two young soldiers standing guard in front of a heavy steel door.

"Mornin' boys." Sampson said.

"Mornin' Sarge," answered one, the other just gave a curt nod.

"Here's the last of them," he said as he spun me around and un-cuffed me.

"Maybe this will all be over soon and we can all get out of this shithole," he said.

The two young men chuckled and nodded, while I rubbed my sore wrists.

The soldier on the left unlocked the door and opened it up. I felt Sampson's hand on my back and he gave me a shove toward the doorway.

"In you go," he said.

The door quickly slammed shut behind me and there was silence for a minute and darkness as my eyes adjusted. Before they could get fully accustomed to the dark again I heard a click. Fluorescent lights blinked to life over head. I don't know what the room was used for before the army showed up but it was a large room with carpeted floors and there was some kind of bathroom facilities set off to the right side. Now, it had been lined with cots and they were mostly filled with men that were beginning to stir.

Chapter 5

"What the fuck?"

"Who turned on that light?

"What the hell?"

"Aw man, why so early?"

I heard all of this and much more as I scanned the right side of the room, my left eye had swollen shut. As I watched them going through their waking rituals of ruffling hair scratching chins or other parts, stretching, yawning, grumbling, I saw only one face I knew. I hadn't seen him in years. He was about twenty years older now and much more haggard then last I had seen him, but it was definitely him. I watched as he sat up on the edge of his cot and stretched quietly before trying to figure out what was going on. He hadn't seen me yet. I started to turn my head to scan the other side of the room and my field of vision was filled with the hulking chest of someone standing directly in front of me. I yelped and jumped back quickly. How the hell had he gotten so close without me noticing? I heard a deep soft chuckle come from him as he stuck out his huge hand toward me.

"Hagerty, John Hagerty," he said as I shook his hand.

"Duncan Mackenzie, and how the fuck did you sneak up on me like that?" I asked, somewhat pissed off.

"Dunno, I've always been good at that," he said with a shrug.

I'm not sure how or why he'd always been good at sneaking around, he was huge. Six-foot six at least, and almost as wide at the shoulders. He had a massive barrel chest and a tree trunk for a neck. His hair was dark brown, straight and hung into his eyes. He was in need of a good shave, but weren't we all these days. He was wearing an old AC/DC t-shirt and a grey pair of sweat pants.

"Wait, Hagerty? Fuck, isn't this your town now? Are you that Hags?" I asked.

"They don't seem to think so," he said, hooking a thumb toward the door. "But yeah, I'm that Hags, and you're Mack from Menotomy right?"

"You know me?" I asked hoping I didn't sound too stunned.

"Of you yeah, it's my job to know who's running what around me," he said, shrugging again.

He led me over to a small sitting area on the other side of the room and I grabbed a seat in what looked to be and was indeed a very comfortable chair. A few others made their way over to us, including the one I knew. I was hoping they could fill me in a bit. Hags sat across from me and he waited till the others got to us and sat as well.

"Hello Duncan," I heard the man I knew from ages ago say as he sat.

I turned my good eye toward him and saw he was smiling. He leaned forward and offered me a hand. Brett Twombly was his name I had known him when I was a child. My mother had babysat his kids almost thirty years ago. He was a local politician so I had seen him around here and there but he hadn't seen me for at least twenty years. The last we spoke was the day he gave a eulogy at my mothers' wake when I was seventeen. I was quite surprised he had even remembered me to be honest.

"Hello sir," I said unconsciously.

"Just Brett, Duncan, no need for sirs," he said smiling.

"Sure thing," I said with a nod, suddenly feeling like a child again at his house in Belmont with my mom.

"I should've known you were the "Mack" causing all the problems for them over in Menotomy all these years. I just didn't put two and two together. I must be getting slow in my old age," he said as he shook his head.

"Hmm?" Was all I said as I raised an eyebrow.

"Umm, let's just say I knew you were always good at finding... mischief," he said with a wink.

"It is a skill I've honed all these long years," I said as I nodded in agreement and smiled.

The other two that had grabbed chairs were Matt Wise and Paul Soter. Matt was the clan head of Cambridge and Paul was The Salem area's chief. I had met Matt once or twice but had never known he was the clan head. Matt was a shorter bald man who had a long grey beard and Paul was tall and lanky with a receding hair line and thick stubble.

"Now that the pleasantries are out of the way, what the fuck is going on here?" I asked.

"Reorienting," Brett said simply.

"Reorienting?" I repeated.

"That or they're just fuckin' killin' us one by one," Hags said

"I prefer to be an optimist," Brett said.

"What is reorienting?" I asked.

"Well the way I see it, they think our patriotic compass is off, so to speak. So, they've brought us all here to reorient us to their way of thinking. That way we can go back and bring our clans back under control," Brett explained.

"Or they're just gonna fuckin' kill us," Hags reiterated.

"Again, you could be right, but I prefer to be hopeful," Brett stated.

"You're the last one," Wise said nodding toward me.

I quickly scanned the room to confirm what I was about to say, "Joe Brunner from Burlington and Marty Whitford from Everett/Melrose aren't here."

"Brunner has been and gone. We think he was the first one they killed," Hags said.

"Killed? Are you sure?" I asked.

"No, no we aren't sure at all. He was here and they took him out one day then he just never came back. John here thinks they killed him, I think they sent him home to bring his flock back to them," Brett said.

"Wow, scared me there for a second. Umm I'm gonna have to go with Brett on this one Hags. From what I could gather I think Brunner was working with or for them anyway," I said.

"What?" Brett asked.

"Yeah I made some deals with him and some stuff just didn't fit," I answered.

"Like what?" Hags asked.

"His meds were fresh, they hadn't expired yet. He also said he had never hit an army convoy. So, if you didn't steal them where did you get them from was my question," I explained.

"Oof, that sucks, makes sense though. He wasn't here more than a day at the most," Hags said.

"He could've made a deal with someone else that stole them I suppose. Putting it all together, it makes sense that he was working with them in some capacity," Brett said rubbing his scruff.

"What about Whitford?" I asked.

"We are pretty sure that they don't care about him or that he's working with them anyway. He's black market y'know so he's probably dealing with them. Selling them stuff as well," Wise said.

"We don't have any proof of that but it was the consensus among us. He hasn't been here either way and we've heard the guards say you were the last of us," Brett said.

"Somebody high up does **NOT** like you." Soter chimed in with.

"Me?" I asked.

"Yeah you," Hags said.

"They fucked you all up. I heard they sent a few platoons to dig you out. The rest of us were mostly just asked to come in. Only one or two of us had to be "escorted." Soter explained.

"How the hell do you guys know this?" I asked.

"People talk. Hell, this is the most socializing any of us have had in like five years. Since we were all here anyway it seemed like a good idea to have a conference and compare notes," Wise said with a shrug.

"Some of us have been here a few days and the guards get chatty every now and again. Since we're all mostly here of our own free will, kind of," Brett said.

"Troublemaker," Hags said as he waved a finger at me with a smirk. "And I dunno about free will, they showed up at my joint with a jeep full of armed guards to "request" my presence," Hags said.

"Okay, so what happens now?"

"Now we wait," Brett said calmly.

While we were waiting I took a few minutes to introduce myself and meet the other clan heads. Some, I had a couple dealings with here and there but most I had never met. We didn't travel very far from home these last few years so I was a bit out of touch. There were around twenty-five as far as I could tell. That wasn't all in the state but I'm guessing anything west of Concord was being dealt with somewhere else. It mostly seemed to be those of us closest to the coast here at good ole Fenway.

After I finished meeting everyone I returned to my seat. Some of the others had wandered off and only Brett and Hags remained. I sat and rested my chin on the back of my hands. My face was killing me. I'd have done just about anything for a couple of Ibuprofen right about now.

"You seem very contemplative," Brett said.

"Ayep," I said.

"Whatcha thinkin' about?" Hags asked.

"Which one of you is right," I answered.

"Does it matter?" Hags asked.

"Yeah actually, it matters a lot. If they just want to "reorient" us then maybe I can lie my way home. If they're gonna kill us, well, I don't think I wanna stick around," I said, as I sat back in the chair.

"Isn't like you can just leave," Brett said.

"Sure I can, if I really want to. No one catches or keeps me if I don't want them to," I said with a smirk.

"No fuckin' way did you get caught on purpose you lyin' prick," Hags said.

"No, no you're right I didn't do it on purpose. I was *hoping* to get away. I could have left with my people before they showed up, but what good would that have done? They'd have just chased us down and I'd have put everyone in danger. I stayed behind trying to stall them enough for everyone else to get away clean. I knew I could've been caught but I didn't want to. Unfortunately, I ended up in the wrong place at the wrong time," I explained.

"Well I know I don't wanna stick around and wait for me to be right. So if you're leavin' I want in," Hags said.

"Killing us outright does no good. They want our people to fall in line. They don't want a bigger battle on their hands," Brett said dismissively to Hags.

"If they killed us most of the people left would fall right in line, except for mine and his clan," I said nodding toward Hags.

"Mine wouldn't fall in line. It'd probably just fall apart if I was gone too long. They're good folks but they need someone to lead them," Hags said.

"I'd like to think my clan would be outraged enough to take to the streets but logically your point has some validity. Maybe we are in trouble," Brett said.

"So how the hell are we getting out of here?" Hags said, glancing at me.

"We're not, yet. This may be my only chance to get close to this new colonel and I'm not passing that up. I like to know my enemy and if I'm lucky I can end this quickly," I said.

"You want to take his measure," Brett said.

"Among other things," I said.

We continued to talk for another hour or so comparing resources, inventory, notes on how we grew or got food. We essentially had a summit of all the clan heads for the first time ever. I discovered that my clan did indeed have the most weapons and ammo while the Salem area had the most canned food, and Hags and his people had the most medical supplies. At the time I wasn't sure what good all this information would be but I figured it could come in handy if we ever found ourselves in a jam. We also bonded a bit seeing as that we all held the same position there were similar situations that we all faced.

Sometime later the door opened and two guards came in. one of them pointed to me and motioned me over to him. I sighed heavily and pushed myself to my feet. He cuffed me before he nudged me toward the door.

"Guess I'll see you all in a bit," I said, as I was escorted out into the hall.

"Hopefully," I heard Hags say as the door closed.

Chapter 6

"Good morning Mr. Mackenzie," I heard from behind me.

I was in a pale blue room that had dark green carpeting sitting in a metal chair in front of a wooden desk. My hands were still cuffed in front of me and my eye had stopped throbbing.

"My name is Major Burns, why don't me and you have a little chat shall we?"

He was tall and thin with a high and tight military haircut. His chin was knobby and his eyes were too close together. He was wearing the standard green fatigues and his boots were shiny. He was probably in his mid forties and he had a big bulbous nose.

"Do you need some ice for that eye, maybe a drink?" he asked as he came by me and sat at the desk.

"No? okay then, it seems that we've been having some disagreements out there in Menotomy these last few months," he said, then paused, waiting for me to react.

"You know, this would go a lot smoother if this wasn't going to be a one-sided conversation."

I just sighed and stared through him. I wondered how long this would go on for if I chose not to talk at all. I figured if I got him angry enough he'd just send me back to the others to stew longer. That was not at all what I wanted, but he was not who I wanted to talk to.

"Anytime now would be fine Mr. Mackenzie."

"I don't wanna talk to you," I said finally.

"That's all well and good sir but you don't really have a choice. Your stubbornness has brought you to us and we need to work some of these things out. Until you realize that sir this is going to be… difficult," he let the last word hang in the air, as if it would intimidate me.

"I'll only talk to the colonel," I said flatly.

"Well, I do apologize sir but the colonel is far too busy to come see you," he said.

"I got time, I'll wait," I answered.

"I have a better idea. Why don't we discuss the issues and I'll make sure Col. Jacobson hears all about it," he said condescendingly.

"Or, you could go fuck yourself. I said I wanted to talk to your CO," I said calmly.

"Are you trying to piss me off sir?" he said through gritted teeth.

"Nope," I replied with a grin.

"Well you're doin' a piss poor job of it," he said as he slapped his desk.

"Just take me back to the others then until the colonel has time," I said with a shrug.

"Listen, we, the US government, was nice enough to let you come in here to air you grievances and see if we could come to some kind of agreement. Considering the fact that you've stolen from us and killed our people I'd say that was pretty damned good of us. If the military were in control like we should be we'd just have you… removed and replaced with someone more agreeable. As it is, you should be thrown in jail for life for the crimes you've committed. So, if I were you sir, I'd take the gift that was given to me and start to realize how

50

lucky you actually are," he said as he folded his hands in front of him on the desk.

"You **LET** me come in here, and the gift? You kidnapped my wife. You attacked me and my people. Now I'm supposed to be fuckin' grateful?" I said wanting to hit something.

"You're still here aren't you? And we're still open to talking things through with you, to help you understand better why we need you to play nice. We could just lock you up or kill you. So I'd say yes, you should be grateful," he said with a big fake smile.

I leaned forward and smirked, "Listen you condescending prick. I don't, won't and never will *play nice*. You have no right to hold me here against my will. Your law doesn't apply here, you have, no authority here. Do you get that yet? You bring me your CO. now or take me back to the others, cuz I'm done talkin' to your ignorant ass."

"We are the law sir and you are still a citizen of the United States of America. Our laws are your laws. So, you tell me what your issues are and I'll take them to the colonel. I'm sure he'll come and see you as soon as he has time," he said as he stood and placed his hands on the desk leaning toward me.

"Your laws died five years ago, when you deserted us," I said as calmly as I could, my hands were shaking.

"Oh!" he said as if a light finally switched on in his head, "Is that what this is all about? You think that we deserted you?"

Fuck, I had let him get to me and said too much, time to backpedal. "Take me back or get the colonel, I'm done talkin' to you."

"See, here's where you're mistaken sir, we didn't desert you. We suffered just as much as you did out here. It just took us some time to reorganize so we could come help you all," he said trying to placate me.

"Fuck you, you suffered. When you don't show up for two and a half years its' called desertion not reorganization you fuckin' prick." I stood up and started toward the door.

"**SIT DOWN** Mr. Mackenzie, or I'll call the guard outside and he'll make you sit down!" Burns said standing and pounding his fist on his desk.

"THEN GO GET ME THE FUCKING COLONEL!" I screamed at him.

"Fine, You sit the fuck down, and wait here while I go get the him. Obviously you're not going to cooperate any other way," he said as he stormed out and slammed the door.

"I tried to tell you that from the beginning you dumb prick," I said to no one as I sat down and shook my head.

Ten minutes later or so I heard the door open. I felt a hand on my shoulder.

"I hear you wanted to see me."

I looked up at him as he stepped in front of me. He was wearing standard fatigues that looked freshly pressed, shiny black boots, a wide web belt with a sidearm attached. He was pale with black hair that was slicked back and very dark brown, if not black eyes, that reminded me of a shark, soulless. He stood triumphantly in front of me and folded his arms across his chest staring down at me with a grin. "You have no idea how nice it is to meet you and how much easier you've now made my life," he said as he began pacing back and forth in front of me.

"You've caused me an inordinate amount of trouble Mr. Mackenzie. In a way you're mainly the reason I'm here. If it wasn't for the manpower and resources you've taken from us they never would have sent me to this shithole to clean it up. So, I would like to personally thank you for getting me sent here, away from my family and any semblance of a life I had back home. I only hope I can return the favor in kind and make you as miserable as humanly possible," he said, all with that same thin smile.

Fucked, I am completely and totally fucked. I knew there was a reason I had a bad feeling about this guy. One look at him and you instantly didn't like him, everything about him screamed douche bag. He reminded me of the kid that was always picked on in school. The one who grew up to be a bodybuilder who was even meaner than anyone had ever been to him. We all know at least one of these guys, hopefully, only one. Unfortunately, this one had control of over 500 men who would kill or die at his whim. Like I said before, completely and utterly fucked.

"Get this prick back to the room with the others. I have an announcement to make," the colonel said as he walked out into the hall.

There was silence on the way back to the room. The guard was behind me and Col. Jacobson walked briskly in front of me. Occasionally, he would glance at me over his shoulder with that smile like he wanted to say something but didn't. As we got back to the room the guard in front of the door opened it as the one behind me shoved me into the room with the butt of his rifle. Col. Jacobson came in behind me as well as the guard who had done the shoving. All the clan heads inside had turned expectantly as I came in. The colonel smiled even wider knowing he had a captive audience.

"Good afternoon gentlemen, I'm Colonel Jacobson," he said as I was un-cuffed and made my way across the room to stand by Hags and Brett.

The murmurs among them started but only lasted a couple seconds. He waited until all was silent again before he continued, "Your man Mr. Mackenzie here, has informed me that none of you are willing to cooperate with us and that we the U.S. government are, to quote him "Go fuck ourselves," is I believe how he put it. Now, that's all well and good. I had been under the impression that you were all independently run, but the good Mr. Mackenzie here has assured me that he indeed speaks for all of you," he paused for a moment and walked slowly toward the door as he let this bit of news sink it.

Brett audibly gasped and Hags just glanced at me. I shook my head at him and mouthed, "He's lying," He turned back toward the colonel with that "What the fuck?" look on his face.

"Unfortunately, that being the case it makes no sense in talking to you individually in our attempts for a peaceful resolution to this situation. Tomorrow at sun up you will all be summarily executed by firing squad for high treason under United States statutes and replaced with more hospitable personnel. This was not the intended or expected outcome but your leader Mr. Mackenzie was quite adamant. I am sorry but I see no other sensible solution. Good day sirs," he said before quickly stepping out into the hall, the guard following right behind him slamming the door shut as he left just as the yelling started.

A few of them just sat on their bunks and sobbed. Even more just started screaming in my general direction while throwing things or hitting something. Three of them charged me as soon as the door shut. I dropped the first one with a right cross to the jaw. The second one grabbed my right arm as I cocked it back and drove me back against the wall pinning me there by my throat. The third was almost on me when Hags grabbed him and restrained him with his arms behind his back.

"Whoa, whoa, whoa!" I heard Hags saying behind the guy he was holding.

"I'm gonna fuckin' kill him!" he said through clenched teeth.

"I… I didn't do it," I choked out.

"Get off him!" Brett said, pulling on the guy that was holding me to the wall.

"WE'RE ALL DEAD BECAUSE OF HIM!" screamed the clan head from Salem.

"He didn't do it, the colonel is fucking with us," Hags said calmly.

"What?" Asked the guy who still holding me to the wall. He had changed his grip though and I was no longer turning blue.

"The colonel lied. Why would Mack say any of that? It gains him nothing," he said as he let go of the guy he was holding.

"For all we know he's a psycho!" yelled one of them from across the room.

"He isn't, I've known Duncan since he was a child," Brett said crossing his arms across his chest.

"Um, can the possible psycho say something?" I asked.

"Oh, sorry," said the guy holding me to the wall as he let go and stepped back.

"I didn't say any of that stuff that the colonel said. Unfortunately, I am still to blame for the predicament we're in," I said as I started to walk around piecing things together.

"You are sincerely not helping your case here man," said Hags shaking his head.

"Hear me out," I said pacing.

"I pissed off his second in command by refusing to talk to him. He went and got the colonel who, oh by the way already hates me, us, this whole place and just wants to be done with it. The way I see it he figures you'll kill me now or he'll do it tomorrow either way he wins and gets to go home soon. Now, if he has to kill some of you to get the rest of us to cooperate then so be it. Like I said all he wants to do is go home," I pondered.

"So we're all still dead tomorrow then," said Matt with a shrug.

"I'm betting if you're still here tomorrow he'll give you that one last chance to go along with their so called master plan," I said.

"Where else would we be tomorrow at sunup?" he asked.

"I don't know about the rest of you but I ain't stickin' around so they can kill me in the morning," I said as I sat in the big comfy chair.

"Oh, now it's time to bust out?" Hags asked.

"Oh yeah it is, I have no intention of playing nice with them or dying tomorrow. Looks like we have work to do," I said starting to put together a plan.

"I told you they were gonna fuckin' kill us," Hags said smiling at Brett.

"Now let's hope **HE** doesn't get us all killed first," Brett said nodding toward me.

Chapter 7

We sat for a couple hours and tried to formulate a plan to bust out before they killed us all in the morning. During those hours the guards brought us some box lunch type food that was very similar to the army's MRE's or meals ready to eat. After we quietly ate what could be one of our last meals, we came to the conclusion that we had no idea how we were getting out before sunup.

We hadn't been here long enough to scout the place for drain pipes or air vents to crawl into. Nor did we know the guard schedule so that we could sneak out during shift change. We were unarmed so breaking out by pure firepower was out of the question as well. Finally, I threw up my hands, "There's no other option really."

"There's no way that plan will work," said Brett.

"He's right, it'll never work," Hags agreed.

"Well, unless someone comes up with something better soon, it's our only option. It's getting late and we're running out of time," I said with a shrug.

"Even if we got out to the field we still wouldn't get far before they figured it out," Brett said as he stood and rubbed his chin.

"We don't need to get far. As soon as I'm out beyond those walls, disappearing is easy. Getting out is the hard part," I said.

"How many of us are gonna go again?" Hags asked.

He looked around and counted the raised hands of the twelve people other than me and him that were sure they didn't want to be here come sunup. Brett Twombly and Matt Wise were among them. The rest decided that they would stay put and take their chances the next morning. They figured the colonel would indeed give them one more chance to change their minds, grovel for their lives and agree to play nice with the government. None of them actually wanted to, but they thought they had a good chance of staying alive by making as little trouble as possible. This group was led by a tall older guy named Art from the Allston/Brighton clan.

The tentative plan was simple but incredibly clichéd. So much so that there was a huge chance of it failing miserably. Unfortunately, it was also the only thing we had come with in such a limited time. The few that were not coming with us at least agreed they wouldn't rat us out and would help us as much as they could. We went over the plan a few more times, walking everyone through their parts over and over. We were only gonna get one shot at this and I hated the idea of having to trust a bunch of guys I had never worked with before to not screw up.

Eventually, I was pretty confident that they at least knew what they were supposed to do. I decided to try and grab a nap. It was still only late afternoon and we weren't going anywhere for until long after dark. Hags told me he'd wake me up at least two hours before it was time to go.

It seemed like I had just closed my eye when I felt someone gently shaking me awake. I opened my good eye and saw Hags leaning over me.

"Time to wake up sunshine, it's gettin' late," he said as he plopped himself back into the comfy chair near the cot I had curled up on.

I rubbed my good eye and wiped away the goop that had collected in the corner of the other. I stood, stretched and heard everything pop and crack. Brett winced and shook his head. I half hobbled over to grab a seat and put my boots back on.

"You sure you're up for this Duncan? None of that sounded healthy," Brett said with a sly smile.

"I'm betting that staying here until sun up is gonna be a lot less healthy for me," I countered.

"Touché," he said.

"I figure we have about an hour or so before they start settling in for the night," Hags said quietly.

I've always hated waiting. It's not that I'm not a patient man but once a course of action has been decided I'm usually ready to go. This waiting crap tends to make me doubt and second guess myself, which rarely if ever works out well for me. I stood in one corner of the large room and stretched out. Old, sore and battered my muscles protested but in the end did what I needed them to do. Brett sat calmly with a few of the others discussing plans for the night and things we might consider for the future if we actually pulled this off. Hags paced, I heard him mumble to himself every now and again but mostly he just paced.

Brett gave me a nod, "I think we're just about ready Duncan, you good?" he asked.

I glanced over at Hags who nodded as well and answered, "Yeah let's get this party started."

Those that were staying behind came over to us and there was much hugging and well wishes between the two groups. I didn't like the idea of leaving them behind but it was their decision and I did understand their line of thinking. It was a logical choice, I just couldn't justify giving in to the colonel's demands.

"Showtime," I said as I watched Hags and the others take their places.

Brett walked up to Art who had picked a spot near one of the middle cots along the wall to stand. Brett approached him timidly.

"I just want to say I'm so…" Brett started to say.

"Shut up already and get on with it!" Art said just before he slapped Brett hard.

I almost busted out laughing but thought better of it as I heard Brett roar and dive at Art. The two fell on the bed while screaming at the top of their lungs. Others joined in on cue as the two flailed at each other trying to seem like they were really trying to kill each other. After about thirty seconds Matt Wise ran over and started pounding on the door screaming for the guards to help and that "They were going to kill each other." Thankfully the guards didn't stop and consider the fact that we were all supposed to die in the morning anyway, and in they came exactly as we had hoped.

As soon as the second guard was over the threshold Hags, who had been behind the door, shoved it hard and grabbed the first guard up under his arms. He locked his hands behind the soldier's head. I turned from pretending to watch the fight as soon as I heard the door slam shut and I took two steps forward. I covered the first guard's mouth with my left hand and slid my right up behind his head. I made a quick jerking motion and heard a sickening crack as he went limp. Hags let him go and he slumped to the ground.

At the same exact moment while Hags and I were dealing with our guard, Paul Soter from Salem and his partner were having a bit more of a problem with the second guard. They got him grabbed and muffled well enough but he was flailing a lot. Paul, it seems, was also having an issue of killing the guard. I glanced over as mine started to fall to the ground.

Paul had his hands in the right place on his guard but he was crying and kept saying "I'm sorry," over and over again.

The guard saw the hesitation and bit the hand over his mouth. Paul yelped just before the guard kicked him square in the nuts. Paul went pale and dropped like a stone. The guard stomped on his captor's foot. He howled, let go and started hopping around. I just shook my head as I stepped in front of the second guard. His eyes opened wide as he saw me. I watched his face turn to rage a split second before he started to swing at me. I punched him in the throat and he made a gurgling sound. I swept his leg and dropped him onto his back right next to Paul, who was still writhing in pain. I knelt on his chest to hold him in place. I snapped his neck with one clean jerk and a really loud crack. I closed my eyes for a moment before standing up and making my way to a cot to sit down.

It was never fun to have to kill someone up close, but it was necessary sometimes. I tried to tell myself that there was no other way and that it had to be done or I'd never see my wife again. That didn't really seem to help much. I took a deep breath and forced myself to stand. I walked over to Hags and the others. Hags seemed fine. The rest stared at me as if they had met the devil himself.

"I'm sorry Mack," Paul stuttered, now standing.

"Fuck off Paul," I said.

I watched Brett put a comforting arm on his shoulder and whisper something to him in the way of explanation I'm sure. I looked at Hags and he gave me a nod.

"Nice work," he said.

"Get them stripped so we can fuckin' go already," I said, killing and incompetence always put me in a foul mood.

"We're on it, shouldn't be more than a couple minutes," Hags replied.

After the soldiers were stripped we put them in the shower area. I put on one of the uniforms. Hags tried to put on the other but it was far too small. One of the other clan heads, a guy named Mike who was from Somerville took the second uniform. Considering we were planning on stealing a truck it helped that he knew how to drive a stick.

We went over the plan again as Mike dressed and I strapped on the gun belt. We both had pistols and rifles now as well as a combat knives and an extra clip each. I felt good having a rifle again but I felt even better having a knife again. I always seem to feel naked without one. After we all agreed on what we were doing, I looked around to make sure everyone was set. There were about a dozen of us that had decided to chance the breakout. About the same had decided to stay behind and call the colonels bluff.

We wished each other well and Mike opened the door. He stepped out into the hall. The others calmly followed him single file and I brought up the rear. I pulled my cap down further, hoping to cover my swollen and bruised eye. We wandered down the deserted hall until we found a stairwell. There were still no other guards at the top so we continued down the hall figuring that eventually we'd find our way out onto the field where they parked the vehicles.

I couldn't understand why things were so quiet and easy until I gave it a minute of thought. It finally hit me that most of these clan heads were here voluntarily. Only one or two had to have a heavily armed escort. The rest came by way of a jeep, a driver and messenger. It seems I was the only one that had to be taken by force. The soldiers here weren't acting like they were guarding prisoners, they had visitors but they more than likely weren't worried about them leaving since until an few hours ago everything was peaceful.

Finally there were a couple soldiers strolling toward us. I saw Mike tense but he kept a steady pace and didn't flinch as they nodded as they passed him. He returned the nod and I heard him finally let out the breath he was holding shortly after they passed me with a nod as well.

"I see some big double doors up ahead. I bet they lead out to the field," Mike said.

"Makes sense, let's try it," I said from the back quietly.

We opened the doors slowly and we all stood there gawking out into what was the bullpen. Beyond that the famous field itself, now nothing more than a parking lot with trucks, jeeps and corrugated steel buildings. Most of us at one time or another had been at this field to see a game or had dreams of playing here one day, I'm pretty sure none of us liked what had become of it.

"Head to the left, near the dugout and get us to that two and a half ton parked next to it," I said after a sigh.

"Let's pray we can pull this off," Mike said as he nodded.

"We'll be okay if we can just get that far," I said as I made my way back to the end of the line.

The field was pretty deserted but really well lit. It was getting on in the evening and there wasn't a lot of reason to stay up late these days. Most of the soldiers were already in their barracks which is what I'm guessing the corrugated steel buildings were. There were a few guards wandering lazily around the perimeter of the field but it seemed like a straight shot from here to the truck if we didn't dawdle.

"Try and look natural Mike," I said softly from the end of the line.

"Easier than it sounds," I heard him hiss.

We got half way across the outfield when I saw a soldier slide out from under one of the trucks. He stood up slowly and stretched, both fists dug into the small of his back. He was holding a wrench and a rag. I saw Mike jump a bit when he saw him out of the corner of his eye. I gulped, hoping he wouldn't blow this.

"Evenin'," the mechanic said with a nod toward Mike.

"Hey," he answered trying to keep it together.

"Where're you takin' them?" he asked with a nod to our prisoners.

"Colonel said we could take this group home since they've agreed to come on over to our side," he said as he kept walking past him.

"Oh really?" he said sounding a bit suspicious.

I watched Mike stutter stop and almost panic but at the last second he recovered.

"Colonel figures we've wasted enough of their time and none of them want to see what happens to the rest tomorrow," he said as he spared a glance back at me but kept moving toward the truck.

The mechanic folded his arms and rubbed his chin pondering the line of bullshit he had just been fed, "Welcome to the right side o' things then sirs," he said with a smile.

Nervous chuckling burst out in the group as we made our way past with big fake grins and waves to the mechanic. He made his way up onto the bumper and ducked under the raised hood. Mike picked up his pace just slightly hoping not to get stuck again. We made it to the back of the big truck without further incident and started to load up our passengers as we heard someone say "Hey" from off to our left. I had to turn my head fully around, since my left eye was still pretty useless, to see the guy sitting in the dugout. He had a pile of paperwork off to one side and a rifle standing against the bench on the other side. Mike swallowed hard and glanced over at me. I whispered to Mike after everyone was loaded into the back, "Get in and start it up, I'll be right there," he nodded slightly that he had heard and stepped up onto the runner.

"Where are you guys goin' at this time of night?" I heard the soldier ask as I jogged the ten feet to the dugout stairs.

"We're just takin' these guys home, they've come over to our side and the colonel doesn't see a reason for them to stay any longer," I said with a shrug, I heard the truck turn over behind me.

"Hmmm, that's odd I usually have paperwork on this kind of thing," he said as he sorted through a notebook.

"Last minute thing I guess," I said as I moved my hand to the butt of my knife.

"Probably, no big deal, just need to make a quick call," he said as he finally looked up at me. I saw the recognition instantly on his face and he started to draw in breath to yell.

I stepped forward and slammed his head back against the crumbling concrete wall as I pinned him there by his throat.

"SHHHH," I hissed as I slid my knife up under his ribs and punctured a lung to help keep him quiet. I yanked it out and jabbed it back in higher jerking it up and in to make sure I pierced the heart.

His feet thrummed on the ground as he died with a low gurgling sound. I pulled his cap down over his eyes and hoped he looked like he was napping. I wiped the knife off on his shirt and shoved it back in its sheath. I glanced around to see if anyone had seen the disturbance and when I thought it was all clear I jogged back up the short stairs to the field.

Mike was watching from the driver's seat and I gave him a nod. I pointed toward the gate and began jogging along side of the truck as it slowly rolled forward.

"I'll open the gate then hop in," I said up to Mike.

"God I can't wait to get out of here," Mike said looking pale.

"Almost there," I said as I hopped up on the runner and held onto the mirror.

I saw one of the gate guards grab his radio off his belt and heard Mike say "Uh oh," almost at the same time as I heard yelling from the dugout 75 feet behind us.

"Punch it!" I said as I dropped off the runner and let the truck slide past me before I jumped up on the cross bar at the back end.

"They ain't gonna move!" Mike yelled as he picked up speed.

"FUCK'EM THEN, GOOOOO!" I yelled as I wrapped my arm in the chain that connected the tailgate to the truck body.

I heard the first rounds zip by my head as the soldier in the dugout had grabbed his dead buddy's rifle and opened up on us. I sprayed a few rounds in his general direction but the truck was bouncing too much to be anywhere near accurate with only one hand.

"Hold on!" I heard Hags say from behind me and felt his massive hands scoop up under my armpits. He quickly yanked me into the truck bed.

The engine roared as Mike pinned it and I could hear rounds pounding into the heavy steel truck body as he flew past the two guards. He smashed the truck into the gate that I had ridden through quietly earlier that morning.

I heard a grunt off to my right and watched as Bob Henkle the Waltham clan head slumped onto Brett's shoulder with half of his head missing. I pulled my feet into the bed as more rounds snapped past and made tiny holes in the canvas roof. Hags let go of me, rolled to his left and covered his head with his arms. Mike was up front swearing and screaming that he couldn't see anything.

"JUST FUCKIN' DRIVE!" I screamed as I popped up and let loose with some more rounds to help cover our hasty exit.

"Where the hell should I be driving to?" he yelled back.

"Head for Mass. Ave. That way we can get to the other side of the fuckin' river!" I said as I unloaded the last of my clip and slammed the only other one I had home.

Chapter 8

We had turned left out of the gate onto what used to be Lansdowne. We weren't half way up the narrow street when we heard the loudspeakers kick in and a booming voice alerted the whole camp to our escape. Mike cut the wheel sharply at the top of the street and we took a hard right that almost tipped us over. I heard the gears grind as he tried to pick up speed and the truck made its way into Kenmore Square.

"Should we try and put more distance between us before we cross the river?" I asked Hags, pushing myself up onto the bench seat.

"Only one way across for a few miles, we took out most of the bridges, has to be Mass. Ave. or else we have to go back the other way down Storrow toward Allston/ Brighton," he said sounding worried.

"We better get there quick then before they shut it down," I said.

We were barreling down Comm. Ave. The truck was bouncing and people were holding on for dear life. I saw us pass the turn that would take you to Storrow Drive off to my right. The truck shifted into a higher gear and I felt it lurch forward. Brett and I were staring out the back of the truck intently, waiting for any sign of pursuit, so far we were clear. We started passing old, mostly deserted brownstones on the once highly overpriced street. I heard Mike curse just before he yelled for us to hold on and I guessed that we were about to turn onto Mass. Ave.

He started the turn to the left and we all were thrown to the right side of the truck bed. Hags fell into me and tagged me with an elbow. I heard others grunt and yelp as they all jumbled together. We bounced in the air as the tires ran over the curb. Mike was trying desperately to keep the truck under control. He was failing. The tires made a dull thrumming sound as they fought to grip the road. I felt the left side lift off the ground. We, unfortunately, were all pinned against the right side of the truck bed which I'm sure didn't help our stability. Some of us tried to shove to the other side of the truck bed but by then it was far too late.

The left side rose higher and higher off the ground. Eventually, gravity had pinned us all against the side of the truck. It almost felt like a carnival ride except there was no safety bar to hold you in place. The engine roared loudly one last time just before the truck heaved itself completely onto its right side. The screaming started as the truck careened through the middle of Mass. Ave. and slid to a stop finally on the other side of the road after hitting an old stone wall.

I climbed over the mass of groaning bodies and fought to get out of the back of the truck. I immediately looked back toward Fenway and saw that it was all still quiet. Our friends in the military seemed to be a bit slow out of the gate. I turned and saw Hags with a few others stumbling out from the bed as well. I had braced myself in the steel ribs of the truck bed that held the canvas cover in place. Others had held onto the wooden bench seat.

We were a bit banged up and I had a good sized goose egg that would be misery in the morning but all in all we survived the wreck okay. Hags had checked on Mike, He had been thrown out of the driver's seat and been hanging by the steering wheel as the truck slid on its side. He had some scratches here and there from the shattering windshield but otherwise he seemed healthy.

"Okay, we all seem to be alive. We can NOT stay here though, we gotta move, now!" I said as I made my way across the intersection to the side of the street nearer to the bridge over the Charles.

"Let's get over that bridge then," Matt said.

"That's no good at all we'll never get over there before they show up. It's too far we'll be sitting ducks," Hags said as he walked quickly toward an alley off to the right.

"Screw that, I'm going home, anyone who'd like to is welcome to join me," the crotchety old Cambridge clan head said as he jogged down Mass. Ave. toward the bridge over the Charles river. Three others went with him.

"No way he makes it over before they show up," Hags said shaking his head.

"He may, he seems to be moving pretty fast," Brett said with a smile.

"Best of luck sir, we'll be in touch soon," I yelled as he got further away. I saw him wave his hand in the air as a sign that he'd heard me.

"Okay, we need to move now, where too Hags?" I asked as we moved into the alley that lead off of Mass. Ave.

"I have a couple places we can go that they don't know about. We can hold up until they move out of the area and then find a way across." Hags said as we too jogged down the alley.

"I think I'm gonna head off my own way actually," said Mike.

"Hmmm?" I said.

"I know a way to get to 99 and that will take me over down near Charlestown. From there it ain't too far to where I need to be," Mike said as he stopped for a moment to catch his breath.

"Yeah we should probably go with him," Paul said as he hooked a thumb toward the Revere clan head.

"Makes sense," I said.

"We'll be in touch soon though. We have a lot we need to talk about now. They'll be after all of us for sure," Brett said.

"Definitely, stay safe and get in touch when you're settled," Paul said as he shook our hands quickly and jogged off behind Mike and Tony Rinaldi who was the Revere clan head.

After making sure they were safely away we made our way down toward the common. Brett and I followed Hags through a couple twists and turns from one back alley to the next. Finally, he pulled up in front of a boarded up brownstone on Marlborough Street and calmly walked up the front stairs.

"There a reason you stopped here?" I asked.

"Ayep, we'll be okay here for a while," he said as he opened the mailbox and reached inside.

"Safe house?" Brett asked.

"Not exactly," Hags said as he pulled a key out of the mailbox and smiled at us.

"I grew up poor down in Southie. I always wanted one of these brownstones when I was younger. So when the end came I sorta just…confiscated one," his grin was childlike.

"Works for me," I said with a shrug.

"Good, let's get inside then," he said as he waved us through.

It was even darker inside than it had been on the street. Hags told us to stay put and he grabbed a flashlight off an end table that he had obviously left for this very reason. He flicked it on and told us he'd be right back with the flashlight held under his chin to make himself look spooky. He chuckled as he wandered off into the dark. We heard him swear a few times as he still managed to bump into something along the way.

Within a couple of minutes we heard a soft hum that I was pretty sure was a generator. Almost instantly after that we saw a light deeper in the house come on. We heard Hags' deep voice call for us to come in. Brett and I walked down the hall as we saw more lights coming on. I hooked a left into what had to be the living room. Hags stepped out of a doorway and smiled. In one hand he had a couple of cans of deviled ham and in the other he had a big jug of Jack Daniels.

"Let's have a bite to eat and relax a little while. Can't really go anywhere for a bit anyway," he said as he sat down in a large overstuffed black leather sofa.

"Don't you think we should turn off the lights maybe?" I asked as I sat in the matching armchair next to it.

"Nope," was all he said as he popped the lid off the deviled ham.

"Won't they see us from the street?" Brett asked.

"Wow, you guys think I'm a moron huh? No, they will not see us from the street. The windows are boarded up as well as covered with plates of steel and welded in place. Oh, and just to make them look pretty there's heavy light blocking shades over them and thick fancy curtains over those. I'm pretty sure the welded shut windows would have done the trick but as you can now both tell I covered my bases," he said before knocking back a swig of Jack.

"Oh yeah, there's also an edge I added to the front door so no light leaks through there either. Just in case you were wondering... assholes, now shut up and relax," he said that last with a smirk and handed the bottle to me.

Chapter 9

We quietly sat and drank half the bottle of Jack before Brett asked if there was a way he could clean up a bit. Hags told us that there was plenty of old bottled water that we could use to wash up but there was no running water in the place. Brett happily made his way into the kitchen.

"You know we still have a major problem right?" Hags asked me.

"Only one?" I replied.

"They aren't gonna leave us be anytime soon. We basically just spit in their face. They're gonna come at us hard now," Hags said sounding worried for the first time.

"Yeah, you're right," I said with a sigh.

"We can't just stay here. They'll tear apart our towns until they find us," he said taking a big swig off the bottle.

"We need to get out of Boston first off and back to Menotomy," I said with a nod.

"Why Menotomy?" he asked.

"Well, we can't stay here in town because we're too close. We need to get a bit of space between us so that we can move around without getting nabbed. We also need to be able to meet with other clans to figure out what we do next. I'm betting they know where your main base of operations is and I'm sure they know Brett's as well. They just raided mine and have no idea where our back up is. So, Menotomy seems like the logical choice of the three," I said with a shrug.

"Okay, all good points. How do we get there from here? They must have closed off the Mass. Ave. Bridge by now," Hags said.

"Yeah, I'm still working on that. I'd have figured we'd have heard more noise though. I haven't heard one vehicle yet go by and it's been like two hours," I pondered.

"What're we talking about gentlemen?" Brett asked as he came back in after having freshened up.

"What to do next," Hags answered.

"Considering that I think the colonel will see this as an open act of defiance and possibly even an act of war, I'd say we have to get out of here and somewhere safe to begin making battle plans as well as recruiting other clans to help bolster our forces. I hate to admit this, but I think we just started something very big and ugly," Brett said as he sat down on the couch and crossed his legs, looking very business-like.

"My turn," I said as I pushed myself off the chair.

"I left a hand towel next to the sink for you," Brett said.

The unlit kitchen was bigger than I expected. It had overhead track lighting with black granite counters, brushed silver appliances and fixtures, as well as hardwood floors. The place probably cost a small fortune before the storm. My boots sounded so much louder clunking across the dark hardwood floors. I got to the sink and found a big jug of water sitting next to it.

I poured water onto the hand towel and cleaned some of the grime off my face. The booze had dulled the pain in my head and made the process much more manageable. I still had to dab around my eye but the pain was tolerable. The cold water felt good on it and just by touch the swelling seemed to be getting slightly better. I took my time while I enjoyed the

74

precious moment of peace and quiet. I washed off my bloody knuckles and dabbed at the cut on my collarbone. It was still sore and looked a little infected. Chris would be pissed if I didn't tend to that soon.

I suddenly missed her very much. I leaned against the counter, put the cool wet towel over my face and sighed. After a minute or so I pulled myself together and headed back into the living room. We were only safe for the moment. We still needed to get out of here soon.

"Feel better?" Brett asked without turning around.

"Much, how're things in here?" I asked as I made my way back to the comfy armchair.

"We were just trying to hash out plans and Hags here was catching me up. You are right by the way. Menotomy is the best choice of the three. They know where we operate and as much as I hate to admit this I never planned for a back up location," Brett said sounding slightly embarrassed.

"See, paranoia has its benefits," I said with a chuckle.

"Speaking of paranoid, I thought I heard an engine while you were in the kitchen," Hags said getting up off the couch and grabbing the M-16.

"Just one?" I asked.

"Yeah, I would think there'd be more, but I could swear it was just the one. Didn't sound like a truck or a jeep either," he said as he made his way to the window.

"I'll check the door," I said as I pulled the pistol from its holster.

I heard Hags grunt from the other room as I walked quietly down the hall toward the door.

"Looks like there's a car parked about thirty yards down the street," Hags said as he peered out the sliding peepholes he had in each window.

"What color?" I asked just before I heard something odd.

"Black," was all he got out before I shushed him.

"Hold on," I whispered.

"What? Are they here?" Brett said as he came up behind me.

"No fuckin' way," I said as I started to put the gun away.

"Is that a dog I hear whining? They tracked us with dogs?" Brett said sounding on the verge of panic.

"Fuckin' dogs? Are you kidding?" I heard Hags yell from the other room. The whining became more intense and louder.

"Just relax, please," I said as I unbolted the front door.

"We're about to get mauled by guard dogs! I don't see how I'm supposed to relax!" Brett yelled as he bolted back into the living room.

"Well, one of us is anyway," I said more to myself than to them.

"Just no one shoot anything," I called as I pulled the door open.

I didn't even get the door half open as I heard the scrabbling on the door frame of the dog trying to force itself inside. I smiled to myself knowing what was coming next. The door flung open and I was bowled over. I was forced to the floor by large furry paws. I heard Brett gasp and Hags curse. It took a moment for them to figure out that I was laughing instead of screaming and that the large dog that was planted on top of me was licking my face not eating it.

"Hi Lily," was all I could get out between gasping for air and keeping my mouth shut to avoid being tongue kissed by my dog.

"What the fuck?" I heard Hags say behind me.

"She's with me," I heard a familiar voice say from the doorway.

I glanced up to see Drake standing in the open doorway with a very nasty looking sawed off shotgun pointing in Hags and Brett's general direction. He had a long black trench coat on and a large hood that covered most of his face in shadow. I pushed Lily off of me and slowly stood.

"Hey buddy," I said to Drake who was now lowering his gun.

"You okay?" he asked curtly, not knowing who the others were yet.

"Getting better all the time, get in here and close the door already, before someone sees us," I said as I backed us down the hallway toward the living room.

"Brett, Hags, this is my oldest and dearest friend Drake, oh and my dog Lily, who as I can see from where her nose is buried Brett, that you've at least been partially introduced to," I said with a smile as I handed the bottle to Drake who took a long pull.

"You THE Hags?" Drake asked as he pulled off his hood.

"I suppose I have to be," he answered.

"Nice, I heard of you," Drake said.

"Any chance we can go home?" I asked.

"Yeah, as soon as you get your slow ass in the car," he said sarcastically.

"Nice to know I was missed," I said rolling my eyes.

"Listen, I have been sneaking around for the better part of a day trying to find you. That tracking beacon in your boot is only so precise," he said sounding snippy.

"You had a tracking beacon in your boot?" Brett asked sounding amazed.

"I believe I mentioned that I had planned this didn't I?" I asked.

"Didn't mean we believed you," Hags said with a smile.

"It'd never had worked if I wasn't smart enough to bring her," Drake said pointing to Lily who was now exploring the crotch of Hags.

"Huh?" I asked.

"The beacon only gets me within a hundred yards. The rest Lily did. I parked in what I thought was the middle of the area and let her out of the car. She sniffed her way all the way up the stairs and started whining at the door," Drake said with a shrug.

"Wow, good girl!" I said as I scratched behind her ears.

"Okay now that we're all happy happy joy joy can we go the fuck home?" Drake asked.

"Sounds like a plan, we're taking them with us. We have a lot to talk about when we get there," I said as we headed down the hall.

"Huh?" Drake asked.

"Oh, we've pissed off a whole lot of people now," I said.

"This is new how?" Drake chuckled.

"It's new cuz this time we're all involved," Hags said as he locked the door behind him.

"Welcome to my world," Drake grumbled.

"By the way, your wife gave Teddy a black eye and she's pissed at you even more than I am," Drake said as he stalked back to the car.

"Nice," I said with a chuckle. "She can be as pissed as she wants. She's safe and that's all I care about," I said as I let Hags, Brett and Lily climb into the back seat.

"It won't be all you care about when you get home and she starts throwing heavy shit at you," Drake said with a smirk.

"It's nice to see you too," I said as we got into the car.

"I know, Oh and by the way… you look like shit," he said as he turned the ignition.

"Thanks," I said with a smile.

"Anytime, hey did you know they turned Fenway into their command post? Fuckers," Drake said.

"Yeah, yeah we saw that," I said as we pulled away from the curb and headed home.

Chapter 10

The slap hurt, watching the crying hurt more. Drake had waited until we were alone to let any emotion out. We had dropped off Hags and Brett at the door of the old hospital and told them we'd be right back after we parked the car. He drove around the side of the building where the car would be well hidden. When we were both standing out by the hood he cocked his head and stared at me. Just as I was about to ask what he was looking at, my jaw and the side of my face exploded. Thankfully, he had kept an open palm because if that had been a punch I'd been out cold I'm almost positive.

"Jesus!" I said as I reeled back a step.

"You fuckin' deserve that and SO much more you prick!" he said, "And you fucking know it!"

"I'm sorry, I didn't see any other way," I tried to explain.

"YOU DON'T GET TO MAKE THAT CHOICE!" he screamed.

"I thought it was the only way to keep everyone safe."

"Fuck you," he said wiping away the tears of frustration.

"I swear to God dude if you ever, I mean ever, pull that shit again and I will put a fucking bullet in you," he said jabbing me in the chest with his index finger.

"Understood," I said hanging my head slightly.

"You wanna take care of them and Chris that's fine but you don't leave me behind prick. Someone has to cover you," he said before giving me a quick hug and turned to walk to meet the others.

"Feel better?" I asked behind him with a small smile.

"Fuck you, and yes," he said, "Oh yeah, I'm glad you're okay… douche."

We were laughing and smiling as we reached the double doors where Hags and Brett waited. Drake grabbed one and I the other for our guests. They were, long ago, glass doors. Now they were covered in plywood and soon to be backed with steel plates. We had moved in suddenly so preparations were still being made. Drake had radioed ahead so they knew we were coming in, plus we had stopped and talked to the guards at the bottom of the hill. They were hidden back away from the road.

As the four of us, and Lily walked into the lobby of the old hospital George was there with Ted, Gomez, AJ, and Chris. He smiled and started clapping slowly waiting for the others to join him in his applause. Everyone quickly followed, except Chris. She just stood there glaring at me. I raised an eyebrow. Drake smiled wide and took a sweeping bow enjoying his ovation. Lily barked at the clapping and circled Chris happily.

"Nice job sir, well done," George said patting Drake on the shoulder.

"Thank you, thank you, I couldn't have done it without Lily the wonder dog!" he said.

George laughed and gave me a hug, "Welcome home!" he exclaimed.

"Thanks George, I hope everything went okay?" I asked.

"Mostly, who's this?" he asked hooking a thumb to our guests.

"Ahh, George, everyone, this is John Hagerty of the Boston clan and Brett Twombly of Belmont. We busted out together," I said with a soft smile.

Chris was still just glaring at me. Suddenly she folded her arms across her chest and let out a loud huff as she stormed off down the hallway toward the old ER. I rubbed my eyes with the heels of my hands and ran them through my filthy hair trying to figure out the quickest and least painful way to deal with my pissed off wife.

"George, please get these guys comfortable and maybe some food if they want it, I gotta, I'll be, yeah I'm just gonna go deal with that," I said as I clapped George on the shoulder on my way by.

"Oh yeah, you most definitely need to deal with that, don't worry I'll take care of stuff here for a bit... good luck," he said as I headed down the hall after her.

I heard him say, "You're gonna need it son," just before getting out of earshot.

The sound of my footfalls were loud as I trotted down the hall, the emergency lighting was all we were burning at the moment so everything was half lit and gloomy. She banged through the heavy wooden ER doors at the end of the hall ahead of me. She had vanished into one of the examination rooms before I came through them myself. If not for the slight swing of the curtain I'd never known where she had gone.

I slowly pulled back the curtain and she was sitting on the adjustable hospital bed with her feet dangling off the side. She had her hair up in a tight ponytail on top of her head and she wore a black tank top with a dark green zipper front hooded sweatshirt, and black sweatpants with her girl sized work boots. She had her face buried in her hands and I could hear the sobs.

"I'm sorry," I said after a heavy sigh.

I walked over to her after closing the curtain to give my very upset wife a hug. She shook me off like a pouty little kid. I tried to hold it in but a small chuckle escaped.

"Fuck you, not funny!" she yelled still pouting.

"Again angel, I'm sorry and you're right it isn't," I said hanging my head to hide my smile.

"Don't you just try and placate me asshole! Drake is pissed too, you coulda been killed!" she said jabbing me in the chest with her tiny index finger. What was with everyone today?

"Yep, I know he was. He smacked me hard to prove it. You can smack me too if you think it'll help," I said standing between her knees.

"He hit you?" she asked, sounding alarmed.

"Hard," was all I said.

"Oh honey, are you okay?" she asked seeming to forget how angry she was suddenly.

"I'm fine," I said with a laugh.

"You scared me," she said as she hugged me tight.

"I know, and I'm sorry, I really did just want to keep you all safe," I said in explanation.

"I wish I could hit as hard as Drake," she sniffled into my shirt.

"I'm kinda glad you can't," I said as I tilted her face up toward me and kissed her softly on the lips.

"You look like shit," she said with a slight smile and tear reddened big blue-grey eyes.

"I keep hearing that," I said with a grin.

"I may not be able to hit as hard as Drake can but I will shoot you if you ever do that again, somewhere painful too," she said as she punched me in the shoulder.

"Great so now you're both gonna shoot me. Why do I even have friends and family?" I said as I shrugged.

"Oh good, he threatened to shoot you too?" she asked.

I nodded.

"Good, now I feel better," she smiled and rocked happily back and forth.

I rolled my eyes and smiled, "I still think I'm going to find out one day that you two are related, the similarities are eerie some times."

"C'mon, let's go introduce me to your new friends," she said before she gave me a quick kiss and hopped off the table.

"I am glad you're okay," she said as we pushed through the ER doors and back into the lobby.

Teddy and Gomez were there with Lily. Gomez was trying to get her to lie down.

"Hey guys, where'd George take them?" I asked.

"He took them to the cafeteria to get them some food and said he'd meet you in the lounge across from it," Teddy answered.

"Excellent, thank you guys, keep an eye on Lily. We should be back in a little bit," I said as we made our way down the dimly lit hall toward the first floor cafeteria.

The cafeteria was on the left and it seemed to be up and running to a small degree. There were lights on inside and I could hear people having breakfast. It was around six AM if I had to guess. I knew we had busted out later in the night and had spent a few hours at Hags place in town, but I have no idea how long or at what time we met up with Drake. It was the start of a new day though it seemed and I was hoping to get a few things settled before I fell over from exhaustion.

I took a right into the lounge and found a big comfy leather chair to sit in. There were leather chairs and a leather couch with a short coffee table in the middle of the room covered with old magazines. I hooked the table with the toe of my boot and pulled it toward me so I could put my feet up. Chris stood next to me and asked me if I wanted a coffee from across the hall. I nodded, closed my eyes and laid my head back on the soft leather.

"Here's your coffee," roused me out of a slight doze.

It was not Chris and her soft sweet voice that woke me up though but George instead.

"Thanks," I said as I sat up and took the cup. I sipped at it tentatively.

"Welcome," he said as he grabbed a seat on the couch with his own steaming cup, "Anyone told you yet that you look like shit?" he asked with a wry smirk.

"Yaknow, you are the first to mention it, I'm amazed," I said sarcastically.

"Glad I could help," he said with a chuckle as the others trailed into the lounge and took seats with their food.

"Nice set up you got here," said Hags as he settled in.

"Thanks, it's the first time I'm seeing it too. I mean first time I'm seeing since we've moved," I said as I took a sip of the warm weak coffee.

"We're gonna need Teddy, Gomez and all the team leaders for this," I said as I glanced over at George.

"I'll go have Teddy fetch them," George said with a nod as he ducked out of the lounge.

He was back moments later and I took the few minutes while we waited to catch up George, Drake and Chris on everything that had happened the last twenty four hours or so. When I was done the three sat there for a moment before speaking.

"So you have no idea what happened to the clan heads that stayed behind?" he asked.

"None," Brett said.

"You know they're gonna come hard at us now," Drake said leaning against the far wall with his arms folded.

"And it'll be all the clans not just us anymore," George said in agreement.

"Yeah I think we basically just declared war. We are royally fucked," Hags said as he rubbed his face.

Roy, Teddy and Gomez all came into the lounge one after the other. Just as Gomez came in through the doorway I raised a hand to stop him from going further.

"I'm gonna need runners, have ten maybe twelve grab gear and wait in the lobby near the doors," I said.

"On it," Was all he said as he spun on a heel and left the lounge.

"Runners?" Drake asked.

"Yeah, we need to talk to the clan heads that are left and find out who's in charge in the towns that stayed behind.

We need to figure out what to do from here. Looks like it's time we had a little clan head convention," I said nodding to myself.

"It seems pretty clear to me what we need to do. We hit them before they hit us," Drake said seeming confused that we hadn't come to the same conclusion.

"You want to put our one hundred, maybe one fifty, up against their four hundred at least?" George asked raising an eyebrow.

"And that's if they don't bring in fresh support," Brett said rubbing his scruff. "Which, I think they will."

"No, we have our little pow wow with the other clan heads and we drive these fucks out for good. We may have a hundred fighters but we have to equal their numbers if we pool the clans and fight as a team," Drake said trying to explain his position.

"Or an army," I said with a heavy sigh.

There was silence for a good long time. Everyone in the room realized that if we formed an army between the clans it was the first step toward turning into what we were fighting so hard against. None of us wanted to be the huge conglomerate that had become the US government before the storm, or the crazy train wreck it was after the storm. I looked around the room. Brett seemed resigned to the idea. The rest ran somewhere between worried to outright frightened judging from their faces.

Gomez came back into the now silent lounge and looked around for a second awkwardly.

"The runners will be ready to go within the hour," he said as he grabbed a piece of floor.

"Let's get the clan heads here to talk before we get too far ahead of ourselves," I said trying to deescalate the panic.

"How long do you think we have before they come after us?" Hags asked.

"I have no idea. If Brett is right and they bring in support we could have up to a week I guess," I said with a shrug.

"So we need to get this meeting together ASAP. If this colonel is gonna go balls to the wall he's not gonna be happy until he's burned this whole place down," George said. "This fucker wants to go home and all he's gotta do is finish us and he can. I'd be surprised if we even have the week."

"Alright," I said pushing myself up out of the chair. "George and I will meet with the runners. Teddy will show our guests where they can get some shut eye for a few hours. It looks like we're in for a very long few days with a whole lot to get done. We'll meet here later on after the runners get back to talk some more."

Everyone murmured in agreement as they nodded and made their way out of the lounge. Drake walked up to me and waited until everyone else had left before he spoke.

"What happens if the other clan heads don't agree?" Drake asked.

"Some of them have to,' I said.

"What if they don't?" he asked again.

"Then we're all dead," I answered.

Chapter 11

I spent the next hour or so working with George and the runners. We were working on who was going where and in what order. I also sent two special runners. One was going to Boston with a note from Hags. The other runner was going to Belmont with a message from Brett. After all the messengers were taken care of, Chris took me by the arm and lead me down the hallway promising George she'd bring me back when the runners started coming in.

As we walked down the long corridor she very clinically gave me a report on the wounded and dead from the attack on the shop. They had gone back at night once they were sure they were in the clear to gather up the few bodies that had been left behind. She took me into an old patient room at the far end of the hallway. Once inside she closed the heavy wooden door. She pointed to the hospital bed and quite firmly told me to lie down.

"Oh I will gladly do as I'm told honey but I dunno if I have much energy to perform right now. As much as I hate to say no to a good romp I'm really pretty tired," I said as I pulled off my shirt and hopped into the hospital bed.

"Yes, cuz the first thing I wanted to do was jump you. Well, normally it would be. Right now I'm more concerned with all the cuts, bruises and that black eye," she said as she rummaged around for stuff to clean me up.

"Some Neosporin, a couple band aids and I'll be fine," I said dismissively.

"Right, let's not forget a couple stitches for that collarbone," she said as she wiped my self-inflicted wound clean.

"It doesn't feel that bad," I said wincing at the sting of the alcohol.

"It isn't unless it gets infected," she said.

There was a quick rap on the door a second before it opened. Anne stuck her head in and smiled. She slipped inside and closed the door quietly behind her. She had on some light purple sweatpants and a dark purple hooded sweatshirt on with some black Reebok sneakers and heavy black socks.

"Oh look who got their ass kicked," she said joyfully. "Was that before or after you got home?"

"Both, most of the bruises are from before," I said trying to keep it light.

"Wanted to check on you and make sure you were okay with my own eyes, she said as she leaned down and gave me a peck on the cheek.

"You and Liam okay?" I asked.

"Yeah we spent the whole ride here laughing at Teddy. Chris clocked him good. Liam thought Teddy was going to cry," she said with a big smile.

"He got you here safe, that was all I cared about," I said glancing at Chris who was threading a rather large needle. "You really should apologize to him some day,"

"Wow, you do see the needle don't you?" Anne asked before she cackled.

"Um, no, I will not be apologizing soon or ever for that matter," she said. "Besides, we've already talked and he seemed fine. He's a big boy I'm sure he can take it.

"He did seem like he was about to cry though," Anne said.

"He really did, didn't he?" Chris giggled. "Okay, maybe I will sometime, but not anytime soon. Now hold still.

90

"Deal," I said as I braced for her to start stitching.

"On that note I'm going back to my room. I just wanted to see for myself that you're okay. Liam will feel better now too," Anne said as she gave me another peck and one for Chris as well before she headed for the door.

"Hey Anne," I said stopping her in the doorway.

"Yeah?"

"Is Liam at a hundred percent?" I asked.

"Always," she said with an evil grin.

Lily meandered through the open door. She made her way over to and sat next to Chris.

"Don't say anything to him yet but we may need him soon," I said.

"I won't, but good. After all this he's itchin' to let loose," she said with a nod.

"He may very well get to do that and then some," I said as I felt the thread tug my skin closed.

"Get some rest. I'll talk to you a little later on," she said as the door shut behind her.

After Chris was done sewing me up, she bandaged it and crawled up next to me on the bed. Lily hopped up into the overstuffed visitor chair in the corner and grunted contentedly. We pulled the blankets tight around us and drifted off for what would hopefully be a very long nap.

I felt the hand on my shoulder and my eyes instantly popped open. I heard George whisper my name and I shushed him. I rolled out of bed as quietly as I could. Chris stirred slightly but quickly fell right back to sleep. It was dark in the room. I nodded to George hoping he could see me. I grabbed my boots out from under the chair and we made our way out of the room in silence. I closed the door softly behind me and blinked a few times to adjust to the light in the hall.

"What's up?" I asked as I stretched and scratched my head.

"The runners are back," George said.

"Good, how long was I out?"

"Probably about five hours, not really sure, I fell asleep too," he said with a shrug.

"Been a long couple of days," I said with a nod.

I padded down the hallway in my socks and turned into the carpeted lounge area. I plopped myself down into one of the overstuffed leather chairs and started to put my boots on. Roy and Lou, the head of security at the clinic, were sitting at a table on the other side of the room playing "Go fish". Dan was in another overstuffed chair reading an old magazine and AJ had curled up on the couch next to his chair for a nap. Everyone but AJ had given a nod of acknowledgement as George and I walked in. I finished lacing up my boots and stood. My back and knees cracked loudly as I did. Dan chuckled and shook his head, never once looking up from his magazine.

"You are getting old sir," he said.

"Been old for a long time Dan," I said.

"So what'd the runners say?" I asked turning my attention to George.

"The clan heads should be trickling in tomorrow morning," he said. "Some said they'd be here first thing some said by the end of the day."

"Okay, so I guess that means we should plan to get things rolling for tomorrow evening. Make sure all of our people that need to be here are here," I said.

"Most of the team leaders are here already. Buck came in a few hours after we got here. Alex came in a little bit ago. Everyone else we've heard from," George said.

"Our current guests okay?"

"Yeah, they're fine. Both of them are out cold. Man, you can hear that Hagerty guy snoring from down the hallway," George said with a smile.

"I guess all that's left is to make the punch and put out the finger sandwiches," I said.

"You think the other clan heads will help?" George asked sounding worried.

"I hope so, I don't see this going well with only the three clans working together," I said with a shrug. "They don't have a lot of choice if they want to stay free."

"True, I just hope it's enough of a reason," George said.

"You and me both, not much we can do about it though until tomorrow, coffee?" I said.

"Yeah, and some food," George said with a nod.

We left the lounge area and sat in the cafeteria for a bit having some weak instant coffee and some canned beans. We caught up on stuff and talked about ideas for the upcoming meeting. Drake joined us for a little bit. He and Sam had been holed up in a room since he got back. I finally decided to call it a night after I caught myself dozing off while staring straight down into my now empty coffee mug.

I made my way back to the room we were in. I quietly slipped off my boots and crawled back into bed to snuggle up next to my still sleeping wife. Lily was lying in the chair, her chin resting on the edge of the cushion, watching me intently. I smiled to myself and kissed Chris on the forehead. I was asleep before I knew it.

Chapter 12

Mike Davids was the first to show up bright and early. I was still working on my morning cup of instant coffee when Gomez came to find me and tell me we had company. By mid afternoon all of the clan heads we had contacted had made their way to our little haven on the hill. Some had come alone, some with small entourages. It wasn't the safest of times to be traveling. Most were faces I had seen before or met at Fenway a couple days ago. A few were the second in commands of the clan heads that didn't make it out of Boston.

We discovered that they had let some of the clan heads go from Fenway when Art showed up representing the Allston-Brighton clan. Amusingly enough, they called them self the ABC's. He filled us in on what happened after we busted out. Some of the clan heads had stood firm and they were not rewarded for their steadfastness. As a matter of fact they were gravely punished for it. Art told me that they killed four of them when they refused to bend to the colonels will. Lynn, Billerica, Reading and Lincoln all now needed new clan heads.

The others only survived because they lied and swore an oath to work with and assist the colonel to bring the other clans under control. This made me worry a bit since they were all here now in the one place the colonel didn't know about. They all seemed adamant that they were only trying to save their own hides. I made sure to mention it to George and Roy so that they could keep an eye on the six to see if they were playing both sides or not.

We all gathered in a large conference room that Teddy and Gomez had set up earlier in the day. There were twenty-five seats around a long conference table. After the usual introductions were made it was agreed that the four second in commands of the clan heads that had been killed would speak for their towns and should be recognized as the clan heads that they now were. They were visibly shaken and understandably upset.

They had all just lost someone who had to be very close to them. In the case of the new Lincoln clan head she had just found out her husband had died in Boston that day. To her credit she steeled herself, took her seat at the table and said she would grieve when the rest of her people were finally safe.

The next few hours were spent getting everyone on the same page. We all at least agreed that the colonel wasn't going to just up and leave anytime soon unless we made him. The problems didn't start until we tried to figure out how best to get him to do that. Most of the clan heads understood that the colonel was going to need to be removed by force. Some though argued that we would be better suited just lying and giving them what they wanted until they went away. Dani, the recent widow from Lincoln, was not one of those voices. She wanted the complete and utter destruction of the colonel. Any other idea just seemed to make her angrier. At least we knew she would fight with us.

In the end, after several hours of debate and discussion, seven of the clans decided that they would not involve themselves in an armed assault against the military. It had originally been eleven clans but Brett gave a stirring impromptu speech about freedom and liberty. He managed to turn four of them around. The seven did agree to help in a support capacity by giving what they could but that they could not afford to lose any of their people. It seemed a bit on the selfish side to me and looking around the room I think many of the other clan heads felt the same.

Late in the evening we wrapped things up and the seven had decided that they would head home to their separate clans, with the understanding that we would be in touch soon to work out how they could help. The rest had decided to stay at the hospital for the time being. We had also decided that we would stage things from here in Menotomy since we were close to Boston and the colonel had no idea where we were, for now.

A few of us sat around the large polished wooden conference table after the others had retired for the evening. We worked out some of the basic details and logistics of all of this. It was tedious work but we had to contact a good amount of people. as well as try to move a lot men and equipment in a short period of time without being noticed by a nearby force. Not the easiest thing in the world to accomplish especially when you aren't an expert at it to begin with.

"Is it possible that this could lead us into a civil war?" Mike Davids asked.

"Anything is possible I suppose but I'd rather not think about that right now. One thing at a time," I said rocking back in my chair at the head of the table.

"It is quite possible that they will send more men if we push the colonel out. It is equally possible that they don't have the man power to send anyone else. All of this also depends on if we even win or not," said Brett.

"If they send more men then we'll just have to send them packin' too," Hags said with a shrug.

Drake had put his feet up on the table he looked thoughtful for a moment and smirked before he piped up with, "What's so civil about war anyway?"

"Dear god, did you really just quote Guns and Roses you jackass?" I said as I rolled my eyes, "Dude you're just embarrassing."

"Heh," was all I got to go along with the big cheesy grin he gave me.

"You're all proud of yourself aren't ya?" I asked.

"Kinda yeah," he said before busting into a loud laugh.

"Nicely played," added Hags.

"I think tomorrow I should head back to Belmont to start coordinating and figuring out what's what there. I would send the runners but my people haven't seen me in a few days and I want to reassure them instead of just sending messages," Brett said.

"Makes sense, I'll have Teddy and Gomez take you over in one of the few cars we have with gas in it," I said.

"I suppose I should make an appearance in town as well," Hags interjected.

"You may take a little more effort my friend. You are, after all, in their backyard," I said.

"There's plenty of ways to get him in town without being seen," Drake said confidently.

"Well then I guess you just volunteered to get him back in then didn't you?" I said with a smirk.

"Fine by me," he said trying to not sound annoyed. "You're coming with me then though. I don't trust anyone else at shotgun."

"Bastard," I said wrinkling my nose as he laughed.

"That'd be good actually. We can check out our inventory and see what we have to offer. I know we have a bunch of guns and ammo, but I believe we also have a bunch of medical stuff from all the hospitals in town. Some of it may come in handy very soon from the look of things," Hags said.

"I guess Chris can go for the trip as well then huh?" Drake said grinning ear to ear.

"I'm sure she'll be so happy too. She's always saying that I never take her anywhere," I said with a nod.

"Good, it's settled then, tomorrow is field trip day!" Drake exclaimed.

Eventually we all went our separate ways. I checked on the wounded then I checked in with George, Gomez and Roy to make sure everything was in order. I found myself a quiet little corner in a comfy room with a couch and a couple of overstuffed chairs. An old flat screen TV was attached to one wall and a print of a man fishing on a serene lake was opposite it. I sat on the old couch and put my barely warm instant coffee on the table in front of it. My elbows were on my knees and I leaned forward. I ran my fingers through my hair and stared at the floor for a good long time. I was trying to wrap my head around what we were about to get ourselves into. How were we going to pull this off? It was well beyond anything we had ever attempted and I was swimming way out over my head.

I'm not sure how long I sat there and mulled things over but it was long enough to start to sort things out. I felt at least a little better. I was brought out of my reverie when I heard footsteps coming toward me down the hallway. The footfalls turned into my room and stopped just inside the door.

"Hello Duncan," Brett said." Mind if I join you?"

"C'mon in sir, have a seat."

"Thanks," he said as he grabbed the arms of one of the overstuffed chairs and turned it slightly to face me.

"What can I do for you?" I asked.

"I was talking to a few of the clan heads after you left. We came to the conclusion that we should put someone in charge of the troops, once we gather them up, since we may be knee deep in battle in a few days," Brett said as he leaned forward while he talked.

"Yeah, I've already thought of that."

"Well, we figured you would be the best suited for the role sine you have much more experience in battle than the rest of us," Brett said leaning back and crossing his legs.

"I'm flattered, I also agree, I'm also not going to be the one in charge," I said with a grin.

"I… I don't understand," Brett said looking baffled.

"Yeah, I thought of that too," I answered. "George has military experience and I trust him implicitly. I was going to let you guys know that he would be in direct charge of the troops. I figured he'd answer to both you and Hags."

"Okay, but why wouldn't you be in charge?" Brett asked.

"My team has something it needs to do and we may or may not be done in time to direct troops or plan battle strategy. I assure you though that George will do just fine and he will be in contact with me as well," I said before taking a sip of my now cold coffee.

"May I ask what it is that you and your team will be doing?" Brett asked tee-peeing his fingers under his chin.

"Of course you can," I answered. "We are going to go in town. Then we're going to find the colonel so that we can make sure he doesn't get a chance to come back and bother us again."

"You're going to assassinate him?" Brett asked sounding shocked.

"Yep," I said matter of factly.

"I don't know if I can condone that Duncan," Brett said sounding like a stern father.

"Good thing I wasn't looking for permission then," I said sarcastically.

"Don't you think this is something that should have been discussed among the other clan heads?" Brett sounded indignant.

"Not at all, this is not a democracy, I don't need to clear my actions with you or anyone else. The man has sworn to my face that he would do everything in his power to make me as miserable as he is. I will not take the chance of leaving him alive so he can come back and put one in my head when I least expect it, or even worse put one in my wife's head," I said, doing my best to remain calm.

"Okay, understandable but still, assassination?" he said scratching his five o'clock shadow.

"Is it really any worse than sending untrained men up against soldiers to fight for their freedom in a couple days?" I asked.

"True, but what you're planning is murder," he said.

"No, what I'm doing is protecting me and mine," I answered. "He made the first threat. I just want to make sure he can't follow through on it."

"I'm going to have to think on this, but I'm pretty sure I cannot condone this," he said as he made his way to the doorway

"Take all the time you need Brett. As soon as I get a clean shot I will kill Colonel Jacobson with or without you're approval," I said before draining my coffee.

"Duncan?"

"Yes?"

"What happened to you? I understand that we've all been through so much in the last few years but you always seemed to be such a loner. How did you come to lead these people?" Brett asked.

"It's a promise I made," I replied.

"To your clan?" he asked.

"To my son."

"You have a son? How come I haven't met him yet?"

"Had," I said staring at my boot tops.

"Oh... I'm sorry Duncan."

"Justin was six. It was about eight months after the storm. We were all filthy, cold and terrified constantly. He got an infection, something so easily fixed normally, we tried everything and it just got worse. There was no FEMA no red cross no one that had any medicine. I searched everywhere for some antibiotics but they had been looted along with anything else of use. He died in my arms after burning from the inside out for three days," I said as the tears bounced off of the leather of my boots.

"Duncan..." was all Brett said.

I cut him off before he could finish, "As I buried him, I swore that I would do anything necessary to keep my people safe. We had basic supplies and had gotten a hold of the guns but we hadn't set up to take care of the rest of the town until after Justin died. At first we made deals with other clans and scavenged as much as we could. There was no black market then, at least none that I could find."

I paused for a good long time before I continued, "They deserted us and because of that my son is dead, along with God knows how many other sons and daughters, all because they were too afraid to come out of their bunkers. I swore I would never trust anyone else with the care of my people and I never will. If that means I have to take out one measly colonel to protect my family and my clan then so be it."

"You were right Brett I never wanted to be in charge. I never wanted to be a leader. After what happened to my son, I didn't trust anyone else to do it," I sighed heavily.

I felt his hand on my shoulder and when I finally peered up at him he looked so sad. His eyes were red and glistening with tears. "I am truly heartbroken for your loss Duncan. I honestly don't know what else to say."

"Much appreciated, if you don't mind though, I'd like to be alone with the thoughts of my son for a bit," I said hanging my head.

"Of course," he said as he quietly left.

I sat there, in the dark, for a good long time after he left. I cried, I laughed. I talked to my son. Then I cried some more.

Chapter 13

The next morning Teddy, Gomez and Brett hopped into one of the pick-ups we used for raiding convoys and drove to Belmont so Brett could discuss things with his clan. They had radios with them so we could get in touch if we needed to.

We had discovered that we could have radio contact a little bit further away now that we were up on a hill. Granted, we still couldn't reach Boston from where we were but our range had increased a mile or two from what it had been. George said he was considering setting up an antenna here if we decided to move back into the shop when this was all over.

I saw Teddy and them off then went to find Drake and round up the others. Drake was coming down the hall toward me putting his curly blond hair up in a pony tail as he scuffed along in his untied, beat up old work boots. He grunted as he passed me and headed into the cafeteria. He found the large coffee maker that was now just filled with water and poured himself a cup. He dumped in some instant coffee and stirred it.

"To this day I never understood why you drink this shit," he said as he buttoned up his black shirt.

"It's just a liquid caffeine delivery system now. I used to actually like the taste of coffee, real coffee," I said with a shrug.

"Yeah, well there's none of my beer here so coffee it is," he said taking a big gulp.

"If we don't go back to the shop soon we can send someone to go get you some more beer from Jimmy," I said with a chuckle.

"We ready to go?" he asked.

"Will be as soon as I grab Chris and Hags," I answered.

"I'm right here so we just need Mr. Hags it seems," Chris said with a smile as she came up behind Drake and poked him hard in the ribs. She was wearing her oversized olive drab coat with the cuffs rolled up a couple times, black cargo pants and her knit cap pulled down tight over her ears.

"You're chipper," he grumbled.

"I never get to go anywhere. I love road trips!" she exclaimed as she bounced around like a little kid.

We meandered down the hall toward the lobby. George was leaning against the old customer service desk. He gave a nod when he saw us getting closer.

"I had Dan go down and wake Hags up, figured he might want to grab a bite to eat or a coffee before he left," George said.

"Excellent, thanks," I said as I strapped on my harness with the cross draw holsters.

"Hey hon, did you bring your gun?" I asked Chris.

"Yep, it's in the small of my back, wanna check?" she asked with a wink.

"If you're busy Mack I can check that for you," said George with all the mock sincerity he could muster.

"HEY!" Chris yelled.

"Just trying to be helpful," George said with a shrug and a smile.

"I think I'll trust her this time, but I do appreciate the offer," I said.

Drake chuckled and shook his head as he pushed through the lobby doors to go get the car. I heard footfalls coming down the hall behind me and turned to see Hags and Dan walking toward us. Hags took a seat on the couch near where we were standing and Dan had a word with George before he turned to go back toward the cafeteria.

"I take it we're just about ready to go?" Hags asked.

"Drake went to grab the car. You need a coffee or something?" I asked.

"Nah, I don't really do coffee but thanks," Hags replied.

"Then I guess we are set then," I shrugged.

"Anyone need to pee before you leave?" George asked as he glanced at Chris.

"Damn you! Now I have to, be right back," she said as she turned and jogged off.

"Bladder of a walnut I swear," I said with a smile.

"I knew she'd have to," George said proudly.

A minute or two later she returned and we all went outside to the car. Chris and Hags rode in the back while I went to investigate the trunk of the car that Drake had popped open from inside. I saw the old blanket and smiled to myself. He had remembered to grab the guns out of the old car that we had pretty well demolished a couple weeks ago.

I unwrapped the blanket and grabbed my AK and a shotgun for him before climbing into the front seat. This car wasn't as nice as the old "Interceptor" in my opinion but it'd have to do for the moment, considering that we broke the axel on the old one.

"Good, you found my present," Drake said as he took the shotgun and slid it down next to his left leg.

"Nice of you to remember to bring them," I said with a smile.

"What's a road trip without heavy weaponry?" he asked.

George leaned on the edge of the door, "You have radios, check in before you leave town and again sporadically to help me test our range okay,"

"Will do sir," I answered.

"Be careful, and don't stay out too long, you know how I worry," He said as he grinned.

"We'll try and be home before dark dad," Chris joked.

He stood and gave a quick salute before he turning to go back inside. We rolled out of the parking lot and started down the steep winding hill that would lead us down to Summer Street, one of the main roads that ran through town. I watched all the dead trees glide past the driver's side window as we slowly made our way down the snow covered hill.

"What, no Sam to see you off this morning?" Chris asked as she flicked the back of Drake's ear.

"Oh she saw me off." He answered with a smirk and a wink in the rearview.

"Niiiice," she said as she rolled her eyes.

"Sorry, you set yourself up for that. Actually, she slept in, been a long couple of days," he said.

Spring was coming but there was still a bit of snow on the ground. The chains on the tires helped but it was still a steep hill to go flying down. We turned left at the bottom of the hill and made our way toward the town line. Drake seemed to already have a route in his head that he wanted to take and since he had successfully got into town to find me it made sense that he could do it again.

We chatted lightly on the ride. We knew we were relatively safe while we were still in Menotomy. We drove past the ruins of the old police station which had fallen in on itself during the earthquake. The road continued on running next to the Mystic River for a short time, before it came to a rotary. There used to be a small bridge that led into Medford. We blew a giant hole in it a few years back so that we wouldn't have to worry about people sneaking into town from that direction. It may seem a bit paranoid but it made tactical sense at the time.

The road snaked alongside the river for another mile or so. I heard Chris sigh heavily from behind me, I knew it was coming. We rolled past a big green house that sat across from the river. It had been our home. Actually, it was still our home. Neither of us had been there for well over a year and a half. It was the house that Chris had grown up in, so she was far more attached to it than I was. She sighed again as we rolled by it. We got off the main road shortly after since it ended as well at another bridge that we had blown a chunk out of.

"I do miss that house," she said sounding very sad.

"I know you do," I said.

We made our way past the old Menotomy housing projects and up onto Broadway so we could get over into Somerville. Drake and I got less chatty once we crossed the town line. We had to start paying a bit more attention to things around us. It wasn't that we actually thought someone would just start shooting at us as soon as we got across the line, but to not recognize that you had just left friendly territory would be foolish.

I checked in with George and he said he could hear me just fine. I guess he was right we would have to get an antenna up there sometime soon. He started to fade out a mile or so further down the road but it was still a significant boost to our old range.

"Where exactly in town are we heading?" Drake asked Hags as we drove by what used to be Tufts University.

"The old state house," Hags answered.

"Really? I'd have thought you'd have picked somewhere a bit more defendable," I said.

"We weren't planning on fighting a war. It's just where some of us get together. We have places all over the city for stores and housing," Hags said.

"You do have a lot more options," I said.

"We also have more people. Unlike Menotomy, we don't control everything in town. We have smaller clans and folks that don't want to be part of any clan at all. I just happen to have the most guns and food right now," Hags shrugged.

We got through Magoun square and were almost through Winter Hill when we saw a group of about ten or twelve men standing in front of an old bar. They stopped talking as they heard the engine and gave us the hairy eyeball. We had slowed down a bit but were still cautiously rolling by when I saw one step off the curb and start out into the street. Drake hit the brakes and I raised the barrel of the AK enough so that it broke the plane of the window. The man stopped dead in his tracks and held up both hands.

"What can I do for you?" I asked civilly.

"You ain't from here," he said calmly. Here sounded a lot more like heah

"Nope, Menotomy, that okay?" I asked.

"Figured as much, Mike said you might be around more often," he said with a grin.

"We're headin' in town, is twenty-eight clear?" Drake asked as he leaned across me.

"Should be, they don't usually patrol down that fah or, should I say they didn't until you decided to bust out," he said with a smirk.

"Yeah, sorry if that caused you guys any trouble," I said.

"Hasn't yet, sure it will sometime soon though. Saw your runnah came in, Mike has us moving to meet up with you guys in a couple a days," he said.

"Good to know," I said.

"Sounds like we're gonna fuck some shit up huh?" he said.

"Better them than us," I replied trying to sound confident.

He just nodded at that, "I'll let Mike know you was passin' through," he said as he turned to walk away.

"Thanks much," I said as Drake slowly pulled away.

We got through the rest of Somerville unhindered. We saw some people here and there but no one seemed to take a lot of notice. I think Mike got the word out pretty well and most were preoccupied with thoughts of what was coming. We only had to travel through a small portion of Cambridge and that brought us by the old museum of science. There wasn't a soul to be found around here, then again there wouldn't really be much reason for anyone to be here.

Route ninety-three ran parallel to this section of twenty-eight and it collapsed during the big earthquake that rocked Boston shortly after the storm. Except for the old museum of science, a small road that lead into Boston, and a few hundred tons of rubble there wasn't much here. Thankfully, the small bridge that crossed over into Boston remained intact. We got over it no problem and headed down past the old Boston Garden on our left. We went up a small hill and hooked a left at the top which brought us up by Boston city hall.

City hall had a large open plaza in front of it and was set back away from the street. The front facade of the building seemed intact but as we passed by it you could tell that the whole rear of the building had collapsed. Across the street from the plaza half of one of the many parking garages had suffered a similar fate.

This was the first time any of us had actually seen Boston in five years. We had heard that there were good chunks of it that were only passable on foot or not at all. Boston was a very compact city with tons of tiny streets. When the fault line opened off the coast the earthquake that followed shook Boston to its' core. Many of the giant gleaming skyscrapers fell almost instantly. Certain sections of Boston were near impossible to navigate because of the rubble that lay strewn about even now.

"We gonna be able to get there this way?" Drake asked as we turned onto Court Street.

"Yeah, we kept the street clear this way, nothing big fell on this end. Have to walk if we were coming up from South Station. The streets get smaller and the buildings get taller down that end. Way too much crap to clear so we just left most of it," he said as we pulled up in front of the old state house.

"Well, we made it this far," I said feeling hopeful.

"Home again, home again, jiggity jig," I heard Hags say as I opened the door and stepped out into Boston for the first time in at least five years.

"Gonna be weird not having to search for parking," Drake said as we walked up to the front door.

"Or getting a ticket," I added.

"I can have someone come out and steal your stereo if you'd like," Hags said as he nodded to the guy at the door.

"All set thanks," Drake said behind him.

"Just tryin' to be hospitable," Hags said as we went inside.

I walked into the lobby of the old, distinguished building and was pleasantly surprised at how well kept it was despite being used as a sort of headquarters. Our boots were loud on the wooden floor as we followed Hags through what a few years ago was a museum. Seems that they had moved all of the displays out of here and it was now wide open. Conversation around us seemed to stop as Hags made his way to the other end of the building.

A couple of guys made their way over to Hags. He smiled and hugged both. The first was almost as tall as Hags and had a similar look to him facially. The one gleaming difference was the shorter guy was very well on the way to going bald. The second man was shorter by a good six inches and had a big nose and squinty eyes. He greeted them both warmly before turning to introduce us.

"Guys, I'd like ya to meet Duncan Mackenzie, his wife Chris and His second Drake..." He waited hoping Drake would fill him in.

"Just Drake is fine," Drake said with a grin as he reached out to shake one of their hands.

"Drake it is. This is Bobby my brother," he said pointing to the tall one, "and Steve, he isn't related technically but he may as well be,"

We all exchanged "Nice to meet yous'" and handshakes before letting Hags take us into one of the offices off to the side. Once inside we sat while Steve informed us that they had indeed heard from our runner and were happy that Hags was okay. He also caught Hags and the rest of us up on what had been going on for the twenty-four hours since then.

"We've sent people to all the armories to take inventory and load up anything that isn't nailed down," he said. "We don't have a lot of trucks but we've filled the ones we do have with ammo, guns and whatever supplies we can live without. They should be ready to roll as soon as tonight if we need to. We been waiting on you to tell us where to get them to."

"Great, I also want to send someone with them to check out the medical supplies we have as well. Some of it may come in very handy in the next few days," Hags said as Steve just nodded and scribbled a note with a pencil on a beat up old note pad.

"Any activity the last couple days?" I asked as I leaned against the corner of an old desk.

"Yeah, they came by here looking for Hags but after they spent a half hour trashin' the place and didn't find him they got pissy and left," Bobby said.

"We put out the word and we've been hearin' back from all the neighborhoods and the smaller clans. They all said they're in and to let them know where to meet up. Most everyone seems to think it's time to get rid of the fucks," Steve said.

"Alright then, I guess we've got some serious work to do then to set this all up. Let's get at it," Hags said as he slapped the large oak desk.

Chapter 14

Hags and Drake stayed at the state house to start putting things together there while Steve took Chris and I down to one of the warehouses a few blocks away. They had gathered a good amount of weapons and ammo that they had collected from the police stations. Some of the smaller groups had gotten a hold of some over the years but they still had a pretty damn impressive stockpile. M-16's, MP5's, Baretta 9mm's and quite a few other makes and models, as well as plenty of ammo for all of them. There was also a decent amount of Kevlar vests as well as riot shields and batons. We told Steve to send for someone with a truck and a few guys to help load everything up before we moved on down the street to where they kept their medical stores.

Chris found a good amount of first aid and surgical equipment we could use to bolster our supplies. She was also happy to find some meds that could still be viable after all this time. Steve said he would have them added to the other equipment that was going to Menotomy. There was also a good amount of canned goods that were stored here. Steve said he would have to check with Hags to see if they could spare any of the food.

BOOM!

We all stopped and spun around trying to place where the noise came from. There were still enough buildings standing for it to echo off of making it hard to place.

BOOM! BOOM! BOOM!

"Those sound like big guns," Steve said looking pale.

"I don't hear them hitting near here though," I said still scanning around and up, trying to find a high place to get a better look from.

"We need to get back to the state house," Chris said.

"Think they're the military's?" Steve asked.

"Has to be, unless one of your smaller clans got a hold of a couple of howitzers," I said as we started to move back toward the state house.

"Man, I hope not," Steve said as we started to jog.

"You're people are smart enough to stay inside through this right?" Chris asked.

"Yeah, of course and those that aren't, they're with someone who is," He panted.

"Kids?" she asked.

"The few we have around here should all be with Kelly in class right now, so they should be fine," Steve answered.

I came to a screeching halt and Chris almost slammed into me, "what'd you just say?" I asked.

"I said 'The few we have around here should all be with Kelly in class right now, so they should be fine,' why?" he asked.

"Wait, you have a teacher named Kelly?" Chris asked Steve as she looked at me wide eyed.

BOOM! BOOM! BOOM! BOOM!

"God, we don't have time for this!" I said as I shook my head and started to run up the street to the state house.

"But, Mack!" Chris yelled from behind me.

"I know, but not now. We need to figure out what the fuck is going on!" I yelled over my shoulder.

"Why is our teachers' name being Kelly important?" Steve asked as Chris gave a frustrated huff and ran after me.

"Later Steve, definitely later," she yelled back to him.

As I came to the intersection where the state house was I saw Drake and Hags standing outside next to the already running car, Hags was looking up at the tower on top of the building. Steve came up behind us breathing heavily as we stopped next to Drake.

BOOM! BOOM! BOOM! BOOM!

"IT'S COMING FROM FENWAY!" yelled someone from up in the tower.

"WHERE ARE THEY LANDING?" yelled Hags.

"LOOKS LIKE THEY'RE LANDING OVER THE RIVER IN CAMBRIDGE. LOTS OF SMOKE, CAN'T SEE WHAT'S HIT BUT IT LOOKS LIKE MASS AVE AREA," we heard from above.

Drake and I shared a look, "We gotta go, now," he said.

I nodded and glanced at Chris who was already opening the car door.

Hags turned to us and said, "You go, we'll get some more stuff together and meet you in Menotomy as soon as we can."

"We may not be there. You have a radio, call us when you get into Medford and we'll let you know what's going on," I said as I heard more rounds go off.

He nodded and put out a hand that I took, "Stay safe," was all he said as we shook.

"Talk to you soon hopefully," I said as Drake pulled away from the curb.

We made our way back into Somerville as fast as we could. We sped up winter hill and down toward Medford. We could hear the barrage continuing to pound Cambridge off in the distance. We were almost back into Medford when I heard the radio crackle. Another half a mile and I could hear George faintly.

"Papa Bear to Baby Bear," I heard him say over and over.

"Baby Bear here," I answered several times before he actually heard me.

"Thank Christ! The fucker jumped early Mack!" George exclaimed.

"I noticed, we're on our way back now,"

"Don't bother, head straight to Cambridge. I scrambled the teams and they are on their way there. Roy has Liam and the rest of Alpha with his team until you rendezvous with him. I'm with Gomez and his team heading to a command and control spot in Porter Sq.," George finished finally taking a breath.

"Roy has Liam with him? Why the hell is Liam out there?" I asked.

"Don't worry Mack, he promised not to do anything crazy, at least until you got there," George said.

"And you believed him?" I asked.

"I was a little busy and short people at the moment to debate too much about it. I'm sure it'll be fine," he said.

"I hope you're right." I said putting the radio down.

"When did he decide to get his shit together?" Drake asked.

"Dunno, but it's kind of a nice change," I said with a shrug.

"Baby Bear, Ratchet should be dropped off at Mt. Auburn to help with casualties. The other docs are already en route," George said.

"Papa Bear, we will drop off Ratchet and get back in touch to find out our rendezvous point," I answered.

"I should have locations for the teams and C and C by the time Ratchet is clear," George said.

"Copy, heading to Mt. Auburn now," I said as Drake took a hard left.

"Copy that, stay safe Baby Bear," he said.

"Will do, Baby Bear out," I replied.

We cut through Davis square and roared up to Mass Ave. Then we wound our way through the old Cambridge neighborhoods until we got to what used to be route two and Alewife parkway. We drove past a lot more people than usual as we made our trek cross country. The world was a much quieter place now and such huge noises deemed investigation. Most people were looking to the sky or standing on rooftops trying to spot the location of the sounds.

Where the rounds were landing was much easier to see. Even though a lot of the larger buildings were in ruin from the storm, the subsequent earthquakes and fires there seemed there was still a good amount left to burn. The huge cloud of billowing black smoke hung over the eastern half of Cambridge as whatever was left burned out of control.

We slid to a stop in front of what was the emergency room entrance to Mt. Auburn hospital. It was built under a parking garage so it was sheltered and easier to defend than the front doors. I hopped out and held the seat forward for Chris. After she was out I poked my head back in and told Drake that I'd be back in a couple minutes. He gave me a nod as Chris and I walked up the short ramp to get inside.

It was chaos inside. It looked like our hospital had just after the storm, an overcrowded ER with an overwhelmed staff. Casualties had begun rolling in from different parts of the city. Some covered in soot and ash quietly waiting their turn while others were bloodied and screaming. The staff did what they could but there were far too few of them to cover all of this. Chris jumped right in, gave me a quick kiss, and found a nurse to point her in the direction of someone in charge. I let her go do her thing. This was what she was good at. Our clan had much more recent experience in treating these kinds of injuries. Cambridge probably hadn't seen this kind of stuff since a year or so after the storm.

I do have to admit that the ER scene was a bit much even for me. There had to be at least fifty people waiting to be seen and God knew how many were already in beds. I didn't see any of our docs yet but I knew they were on the way. I just hoped it was going to be enough.

I finally got the attention of one of the people doing triage in the lobby and asked where I could find Matt. They told me that he was up in the main lobby and hastily pointed me to the closest stairwell. I said thanks over my shoulder and quickly made my way upstairs to the lobby.

The lobby had multiple entrances and I found Matt with some of his people by the glass doors that overlooked the nearby Charles River. He was having a fairly heated discussion with two men when he noticed me. He instantly stopped what he was doing and came toward me. His already old face seemed

120

more haggard than the last time I had seen him only a couple days ago.

"Thank you Mack, I'm so glad you're here," he said profusely shaking my hand.

"My wife is down stairs helping out with your staff. The rest of our docs are on the way," I said.

"Yes, yes George told me. We sent a radio man to the city line. He was relaying messages back and forth when the shelling started. I believe your people are now in the city so we can speak directly to them," Matt said.

"Good, that will make things easier, I'm going to head over to where George is in a minute but I wanted to check in with you first to see if there was anything I needed to know," I said looking out the glass doors to watch the dark grey sky.

"It seems that the shelling has stopped for now but I have reports of troops coming across the Mass Ave. Bridge," he said sounding worried. "They tell me that they are demanding the surrender of all arms to them and that we clan heads turn ourselves in to them within two hours or there will be more shelling."

"He really is just pulling out all the stops now isn't he?" I said to myself as I shook my head. "Okay, I'm gonna go and meet up with my teams to see if we can't stop this. Gather up as many men and weapons as you can. Send them over as soon as possible. Oh, and call George and tell him what you just told me."

"I will. I don't know how many people I can find or spare that quickly but we'll do what we can," Matt said. "Stay safe Mack."

"Dunno how well I can do that today but thanks," I said as I pulled open the heavy steel door that lead back to the stairwell.

Back downstairs I found Chris working triage with a few others. I pulled her aside quickly and told her I was leaving. She nodded, kissed me hard on the lips and told me she loved me. She spun around and ran back into the fray. I worked my way through the crowd of wounded and found Drake still sitting right outside the doors ready to go.

"Looked like hell in there," he said as he drove up the exit ramp.

"Yep, pretty much," I agreed.

I keyed the mic and called George. He told me that he was set up in porter square and where I could find him. I wasn't really surprised when he told me they had set up in the old Uno's there. He did have a half way decent reason. It was on the second floor so he would have a better line of sight and range. I let him know that we'd be there shortly. Just before he signed off he told me to switch over to the ear buds when we came through Harvard Square. They had a shorter range but there was less chance of our conversations being heard.

We traveled up Mt. Auburn Street and I filled Drake in on my conversation with Matt while we drove. We stopped before we got to Mass Ave. and made sure that the troops hadn't gotten that far before we popped out and backtracked to Porter.

George had set up shop on the second floor of one of the buildings in Porter Square. It used to be a decent pizza shop that overlooked the train station. It was back far enough away from Mass Ave. that they wouldn't be easily seen. Gomez and his team had finished setting up just a few minutes before we arrived.

We parked around the back side of the building on the second floor of a small parking garage and found one of our men at the back door as we went in. He told us that George was up front and expecting us. When we found him George was sweating profusely and looked worried.

CHASE/AFTER THE STORM BOOK 2

"We have a problem," he said as we came into the old restaurant.

"Only one?" Drake asked sarcastically.

"I only know where some of the teams are. I can't get in touch with Cain or Jay. I don't know whether it's an equipment issue or they're something worse," George said.

"Alright, give us the location of who you do know and we'll check the others when we get there," I said as I stowed some extra clips in the side pockets of my black cargo pants.

"Here," he said as he handed me a piece of paper out of a notebook, "I've already written them down. Now get out there and let me know who's safe and who isn't," George said.

"We're on it," I said as Drake and I turned to leave.

"Good hunting," George said as we walked back out.

All was quiet until we got past Harvard square. The smell of burning got much stronger the further we went. The acrid smoke started to burn our eyes as we decided to leave the car and walk the rest of the way just outside of Central Square. Drake and I both covered our mouths with black kerchiefs to help filter out some of the smoke, making us look like old western bad guys. I shrugged out of my long coat and tossed it in the back seat. We both carried AK's, pistols and plenty of spare ammo. Drake had a shotgun slung across his back and I had a backpack full of spare clips incase our boys were running out.

Inky black pillars of smoke rose into the afternoon sky ahead of us as buildings further down Mass Ave. burned. Roy's team and alpha were hole up in an Irish pub right at the edge of the old MIT campus according to George's information. We stayed to the right hand side of the road. As we got closer we could hear the sounds of gunfire further up. We picked up the pace and jogged the rest of the way to the pub. I expected a full-fledged fire fight by the time we showed up but it was all clear outside the pub. The gunfire was coming from further down Mass Ave. somewhere on the MIT campus.

Drake and I each took a side of the door leading into the pub. He pulled the heavy wooden door open. I leaned in and gave a shout to let them know we were there. I heard Roy give us the all clear and we ducked inside. Both teams were over by the window that faced out to the street. Long ago it was a thick plate glass, now just an empty hole in a deserted building.

"Glad you could make it," Tom joked.

"We didn't want you guys to have all the fun," Drake retorted as he gave him a quick hug.

"'Bout time you two showed up. I told George I wouldn't do anything stupid until you got here," Liam said grinning.

"Please don't do something stupid now that I am here," I said.

"For now," was all he said.

"Who's doing the fighting?" I asked Roy with a sigh.

"Right this moment Jay and Buck's teams along with some of the Cambridge citizens that decided to hand over their weapons one bullet at a time. They are the closest ones to the bridge," he told me.

"So Jay and Cain are okay so far?" I asked.

"So far, they had some bad equipment and I guess George can't hear them. They can hear him though," he answered.

I nodded, keyed my mike and filled George in. After that I called Buck to see how they were doing. Buck told me they were getting a bit low on ammo but that everyone was safe. After checking in I figured it was time to get to work.

"Alright, let's get out there and move a couple of these cars across the road so we have some cover when they get here. It'll also make it a lot harder for them to just drive on through here," I said as the two teams nodded and made ready to move out.

About thirty yards away from the front of the pub there was an old car that was already sitting half on the sidewalk and half in the street. We adjusted it slightly and found another nearby to move into place effectively cutting off one side of the street. It wouldn't prevent the troops from coming through completely but it would slow them down. The two cars also gave great cover for Alpha. Roy's team was going to set up in one of the buildings across the street that wasn't burning.

The gunfire up ahead was getting louder and more sporadic. Buck gave a call and said that his and Jay's teams were falling back and were almost out of ammo. There were other teams between them and us but I called the two that were closest to them and told them to fall back as well. I wanted to consolidate our firepower so that we could ambush them from all sides at once and hoped that we could send them packing quickly without a lot of death on either side.

Within a few minutes I could hear by the radio chatter that Jay and Buck's teams had met up and fallen back a couple blocks to a building that was about seventy yards from our location. They were continuing to come back further but needed to stop to take care of one of their wounded. It seems that most of the Cambridge citizens that had joined in with them earlier had stayed behind to keep a group of soldiers pinned down. The rest of the teams had set up within a one block perimeter of where we were and ready to go. We had set up in a horseshoe shape with Alpha, behind the cars, closing it all off. According to Buck, the troops were advancing along Mass Ave. They were trailing his team, and harassing them with light fire.

125

We could see the first of the troops ducking in and out of cover as they came toward us. Buck radioed me to let me know they were on the move again and they were coming in hot. He would meet up with the outermost team. He'd leave Jay's team and the wounded there before moving the rest of his team toward Roy to bring the troops further in.

There was a large gap that they had to cross to get to the outermost team. I held my breath as I saw Jay and Buck break cover, running for the other side of the street to set up and give cover fire for the rest of their teams. Gunfire erupted when they were little more than halfway across and they both dove. They scrambled the rest of the way before returning fire. They laid down cover fire as the two teams crossed as quickly as they could. From the glance I got, they had two wounded that were being carried and three or four that were limping/running under their own power.

There looked to be a good thirty to forty troops running them down. I don't know how many the Cambridge folks had pinned down, but I knew there were at least another sixty to seventy that were still behind this group. It seems the colonel hadn't sent all of his troops, which is good considering they'd have slaughtered us in ten minutes flat if he had. I had to remind the outer teams not to fire at the troops yet so they wouldn't give away our positions. The troops thought they were chasing locals that had no idea what they were doing and I wanted them to think that right up until it was too late.

Buck broke cover with four of his men and ran down the sidewalk toward us. They made it about halfway to Roy's team and had to dive for cover as the troops opened up on them from the edge of our block. Buck poked his head out and returned fire trying to draw them further in. When the troops realized they had Buck's team pinned down they slowly advanced down the opposite side of the street until they were directly across from Buck and his men. They took up positions behind a short wall just back from the sidewalk.

Buck called to tell me they were almost out of ammo and I had to have him repeat it three times because the gunfire was so loud. The troops were riddling his cover and they couldn't hold out much longer. I was just about to let him know that they didn't have to wait long when I heard Liam roar and AJ yell for cover fire. I spun in confusion and saw AJ stand with his M-60 and open up on the troops fifty yards away.

"AJ, NO!" I yelled as I dove toward him.

We were all crouched behind the cars and I had to shove past Tom and Drake to get to him. He couldn't hear me over the roar of the sixty and Liam who was running toward the entrenched troops. Hearing the chugging of the machinegun, half of them instantly spun and opened fire in our direction.

I looked up and saw fear on AJ's face a split second before he took two in the chest. He staggered backwards a step or two still banging away with his sixty. I reached out and grabbed his pant leg just as I saw his head snap back and his brains paint the asphalt behind him. The sixty fired straight up in the air as he fell back with a thud behind the car then went silent.

There was a long moment where everything went far away and I couldn't see or hear anything except AJ and his final gurgling breath. He was already dead but his body convulsed a few times as I screamed his name over and over again. My own voice sounded tinny and hollow. I pulled him into my lap and cried. I know I was saying something but I have no idea what it was. I finally felt Drake grabbing at me trying to pull me back into the moment. I stared at him blankly while he shook me screaming that it was falling apart and the George was calling. I blinked a few time and took a last look at my old friend.

"He's dead Mack!" I heard him yell finally, "George says that Hags is on his way with more men and should be here in about five minutes."

I nodded in vague understanding. I heard Liam roar a short distance away. I poked my head around the edge of the car and saw that he was about twenty yards away behind the back end of a Volvo with four flat tires. He was trying to keep the troops pinned down. I felt a rage well up in me and bolted around the corner. Drake yelled after me before he and Tom gave me cover fire.

Liam was sitting with his back against the trunk of the Volvo. He smiled as he saw me running toward him, it quickly faded and he tilted his head in curiosity when he saw my face. I dove the last few feet and landed on his outstretched leg. I reached out and bashed his head against the solid steel of the trunk. He grunted and grabbed me by the throat as I swung connecting with his jawbone.

"**YOU FUCK!**" I Screamed as I swung again. "**YOU FUCKIN' KILLED AJ YOU PRICK!**"

"**WHAT THE FUCK?**" he yelled back trying to fend off my blows.

"**MACK, YOU HAVE INCOMING!**" I heard Drake yelling in my earpiece.

"**I'LL DEAL WITH YOU LATER FUCK!**" I yelled as I rolled off of him.

"I still don't understand…" Liam tried to say but I cut him off.

"Later douchebag, we've got company," I said as I poked my head around the edge of the Volvo.

There were five or six troops crouched and making their way to us. The rest of the teams had opened up. The troops behind the wall were being kept busy trying to hold their position. As I had suspected they were joined by another forty or fifty men now and were rapidly trying to set up a counter to our ambush.

I grabbed Liam's AR-15 that he had dropped when I jumped him and fired around the edge of the car at the oncoming troops. I saw one go down and felt the barrel of the rifle swing wide as one of the troops kicked it out of my hand. He drew back again and tried to kick me as I grabbed his boot. I yanked upward as I stood. He fell back and I drew my Sig firing two into his chest just before the third caught me high on the shoulder with the butt of his rifle. I dropped the Sig and spun back in time to see Liam come from behind the car slamming the one who had just hit me into the wall of the building next to us. He tore the helmet off the troop and smashed his head repeatedly off the stucco wall.

I pulled my other gun out of the holster and took out the next two as they were training their weapons on Liam who was still pummeling their friend. The last spun on me and fired a burst that went wide as I emptied the clip into him. I pulled the trigger over and over again until the slide locked back. Liam let the soldier he had been finishing off drop to the ground and we quickly made our way back to the relative safety of Alpha's position.

"You fuckin' stay here and don't do anything unless I tell you to. Do you understand?" I said through gritted teeth as I pointed to a spot next to AJ's body.

Liam just nodded and sat down next to AJ staring sadly at his lifeless body. The troops had been hard pressed by the teams and were now starting to withdraw from behind the low wall. I heard engines and was relieved to find Hags in a Ford F150 along with five other pickups filled with men rolling toward us. They stopped about ten yards behind us blocking the street entirely. The men emptied into the streets taking up positions behind them.

The troops saw the extra men arrive and withdrew even faster. When Hags' men opened up along with our teams, the troops fled to their previous position for a short time before withdrawing further. Within twenty minutes the gunfire had died down to almost nothing. Hags' men and three of my teams steadily moved them back toward Boston. Ten minutes later the last of the troops had retreated to beyond the Mass Ave. Bridge that spanned the Charles River. We had pushed them back for now but at a huge cost to me and my teams.

Chapter 15

I could hear the celebration off in the distance. Men and women yelling, screaming, hooting and hollering at the fact that they had just pushed back an enemy force that they didn't think they could stand up to. They were jubilant, terrified and filled with adrenaline all at once. More than a little ammo was wasted when a bunch of them all decided to let loose and fire straight up in the air to celebrate.

Tom, Drake and Liam had gone to check on the other teams as well as help gather the wounded and the dead. My teams were not celebrating. For them it was just a continuation of what we had been doing for the last two and a half years, on a much larger scale. We had lost three of our own today. For us there was no reason to party.

I sat with my back against an old car and stared blankly at nothing next to the body of a dear friend. I pulled the kerchief down and let it hang around my neck as I dug the heels of my palms into my eyes. I couldn't get the look of abject fear on AJ's face out of my head. I knew that this wasn't my fault and that men die in battle, but I sure as hell didn't have to like it.

Drake made his way over to me and plopped himself down next to me. He pulled down his kerchief as well and gave a big sigh as he thudded the back of his head against the metal of the car door. He quickly stopped and I could feel him watching me before I turned to him. The top half of his face was covered with soot and the bottom that had been covered by the kerchief was nearly pristine. Any other time and I'd have been much more amused by this.

"Do I look as silly as you do?" I asked in a dull monotone.

"Yep," he replied.

"Lovely," I said.

I went back to staring between my feet and he did the same for a short time. He broke the silence by asking me if I was okay. I saw him nod out of the corner of my eye as I told him yeah. He stood then and I glanced up to see him holding out a hand to help me up. I took it with a small smile as he pulled me up and into a hug. I only felt marginally better when I heard him tell me it wasn't my fault.

Hags and some of his men were on their way back from the bridge when he saw Drake and I and broke off from them to come over to us. His large grin faded when he saw that we were standing next to a body. He held up a finger and jogged over to his truck. He disappeared inside for a moment and emerged holding a blanket that he brought over. He solemnly covered AJ with.

"Thank you for that," I said.

"No problem," he said.

"Let me give you a hand, we can put him in the bed of the truck," Hags said.

"We got it," Drake said.

"I understand," Hags said taking a step back.

"Are we just about ready to pack up?" I asked as I glanced back and forth between them.

"Yeah, Roy and a few others went to grab the trucks. Liam and the teams are over at the pub waiting for them," Drake reported.

"My men are just about done as well. They are wandering back from the bridge now. We should be good to go in about fifteen," Hags said.

"I'm glad you showed up. I wasn't sure how that one was gonna turn out," I said.

"Glad we could make it. What's the plan now?" Hags asked.

"Yaknow, I'm not actually sure yet. I know the colonel reacted faster than we thought he would but I think this was his way of testing the waters. I think we have a couple days now, so we should continue to gather our forces and supplies. I'm gonna have some men stationed down here so we don't get surprised again. Beyond that though I have no idea yet," I said pacing slowly and running a hand through my hair, "I need to bury my dead and try to clear my head before I make any decisions."

"Sounds good," Hags said.

"We're gonna swing by Mt. Auburn before heading out of town to have some of our men treated since all of our docs are there helping out," I said.

"I'll send my men back in town with Steve and I'll follow you over there with my brother," Hags said.

Roy came around the corner driving a beat up old pick-up in front of the other vehicles that transported our teams here. Most of the time we liked to use bikes since fuel is a pretty rare commodity these days, but every team did have a vehicle fueled at all times in case of an emergency. I'd say today counted. The other trucks and vans parked in the road waiting for their respective teammates to climb in. Roy came to us and together we put AJ into the bed of the pick-up. The rest of Roy's team climbed in carefully after. I closed the tailgate on Roy's truck. Drake and I climbed up onto the back bumper and held on while Roy drove us down Mass Ave. to where we had parked the car.

"We'll meet you at Mt. Auburn?" Roy asked.

"Yeah, we'll be right behind you. Go through Harvard Square to get there. I don't want us traveling along the river.

The colonel doesn't know that they are using Mt. Auburn and I wanna keep it that way," I said as I stood behind the open car door.

"Got it, I'll let the others know. See you in a bit," he said with a wave as he pulled off.

I leaned on the top of the door and looked off into the distance where some of the buildings of Cambridge still burned. Pillars of smoke still trailed off into the already grey sky. Drake saw that I was spacing out and hopped up onto the hood of the car. He busied himself by retying his boots. He pulled his hair out of the ponytail it was in and shook his head to loosen it. He slid down off the hood of the car and rolled up the sleeves of his black button up shirt as he made his way to the driver side door.

"You 'bout ready to go Nero, or did you want to watch the rest of Rome burn?" he asked as he got into the driver seat.

"Yeah, I suppose. Sorry was just zoning," I said as I tossed my rifle in the back and got in.

"Really, I hadn't even noticed," Drake said straight faced.

"Let's go see how Chris is doing," I said.

"Gotta be better than we are," he said as we pulled away.

We walked in the doors to the ER at Mt. Auburn to find a madhouse. More wounded had poured in during the battle. Roy and the teams had added our wounded to the already over worked staff. We stopped at the front desk and waited a good five minutes before we could ask the frazzled girl at the desk if she knew where Chris was. She just pointed to the two heavy wooden doors that separated the waiting room from the actual ER itself and moved on to the next person waiting for her attention.

As we pushed through the doors we could hear the moaning, screaming and crying of the wounded and dying inside. Chris saw us walk in and she made her way quickly toward us. She had changed into scrubs that were now stained with a good amount of blood and her hair was tied back. She was sweaty and pale. She peeled the latex gloves she had on and tossed them onto the floor.

"Good you're here, Roy told me you won," she said as she wiped her forehead with the back of her hand.

"We got them back over the bridge, I dunno if I'd call it a win," I said.

"Well you're here safe. I'd call that a win," she said as she leaned up and gave me a quick kiss.

I took a deep breath and before I could tell her about AJ she cut me off, "Can I get you and a couple teams to help me out here if you're done with the bad guys?" she asked.

"Sure, we are yours to command," I said trying to force a smile.

"Good, you two can start grabbing patients from triage. Have your teams find me so I can get them doing laundry and changing beds. I can't really spare the medical people to do all that right now," she said as she snapped into business mode.

For the next eight hours I got to follow for a change. We moved patients, refilled supplies, made beds and even assisted in some minor procedures. I think at one point I saw Roy stitching up one of his guys. It was nice actually just doing what I was told and not having to scrutinize it. I watched Chris run some other clans ER flawlessly. They had a chain of command in place but their doctors didn't have as much experience with battle wounds or mass overflow. Chris did and she was good at it. The girl at the desk told me later in the day that Chris had barely been there an hour before the Mt. Auburn

135

doctors started coming to her with questions and turning to her to run triage. From what I could tell she was much better at running things here at the hospital than I was out in the field.

It was dark out by the time we actually got to sit and have a cup of instant coffee. Chris had told us to take a break when things had slowed down a bit. The extra help had freed up some nurses and doctors to get caught up. We collapsed into the overstuffed leather chairs in the lounge at the far end of the ER.

I had sent most of the teams and Liam back to Menotomy. My team and Roy's had stayed here to help out. Keith's team was heading over to the Cambridge side of the bridge to keep an eye on things and give us a heads up if anything happened. I'm sure I could have had some of the locals do the job but I'd rather have men I trust out there.

Chris came into the room half way through my cup of coffee and she flung herself down on the couch at the end of the room near the boarded up window. All the air rushed out of her in a giant "OOOOF" as she hit the leather sofa cushions. She lay there for a short time with her eyes closed, her thumb and forefinger pinching the bridge of her nose.

"How you doin'?" Drake croaked still slumped in his seat.

"I haven't had a shift like that since right after the storm. Then again, I could just be getting old," she said with her eyes still closed.

"Probably the latter," Drake said with a weak grin.

"Thanks," Chris mumbled.

"Is everyone safe and sound?" Roy asked.

"Some of their docs are patching up the more minor wounds now, so yeah, everyone is safe. We lost some today but we saved a lot more," she said. "All in all I'd have to say it was a win all around today.

"Cheers to that," Roy said as he raised his coffee mug.

"Mack, I think I should probably stay here tonight in case they need me for something," she said her eyes still closed.

"Already thought of that, I talked to Matt before I finally sat down and he's got some spare rooms for us. George came in a while ago and was setting up his command post on one of the upper floors. This way we can keep in touch with Hags' guys in town." I said.

"Yeah, you do realize I heard nothing after 'he's got some spare rooms for us,' right?" she asked as she got up off the couch and stretched.

"I do now," I said with a grin.

"Okay tough guy, show me where I get to go night night," she said, as she grabbed my hand and pulled me up out of the comfy chair.

"Guys, I'll be back after I…" I said.

"No, no you won't be back. Sorry boys. Doctor says he needs to go to bed. Unless something explodes he'll see you all in the morning," Chris said as she headed for the door.

There was a smattering of tired laughter and a chorus of "goodnight" as we made our way into the hall. Suddenly she stopped and turned to poke her head back into the door.

"Those doctors' orders for sleep apply to all of you as well, and I'm serious. It's been a very long day for everyone and you all need to rest because I don't think it's going to get better any time soon so go to bed while you can," she said.

"Yes mom," Drake yelled as she grabbed me and continued down the hall.

We found a room on the third floor that was empty and slipped inside. We quickly locked the door and stripped down before climbing into bed. There was a half assed attempt at trying to get something going but I gave up the thought of that when I heard a soft snore coming out of my dear wife who had somehow managed to fall asleep mid kiss. I chuckled to myself, shook my head and was asleep before I knew it.

Chapter 16

It had been a long day so far and it was probably only ten AM. I had been meeting with Matt Wise and Hags from about halfway through my first cup of coffee. Then Brett and a few other clan heads from nearby towns had shown up. Evidently, George had taken it upon himself to send out runners after the battle to fill them in on what had happened.

We all sat and talked for awhile. Brett and the others told me they could have some men here in Cambridge by the end of the day, but that supplies would take a little longer. I tried to assure them that we had at least a couple days to prepare before the colonel tried anything again. He had just lost more than a dozen men and would think twice about throwing more lives away carelessly when they were so hard to replace. We discussed logistics and transport for a bit longer before we parted ways and got back to business. I told Matt that I was going to take my dead home to give them a proper burial but that we would be back sometime that night to see how much progress had been made.

"So, I suppose we should start referring to you as General Mackenzie," Brett said as I stepped into the stairwell.

"You could if we were an army, but considering we aren't I'd have to strongly suggest against it," I said hoping to sound annoyed.

"What do you think we are rounding up now if it isn't an army?" he asked.

"Listen, I'm on my way home to bury three very good friends, one of them because I couldn't control my own damn people. You think we could possibly talk about this when I feel more like a leader and less like an idiot for even getting involved in all this?" I said as I spun and started back down the stairs.

"You're right, sorry bad timing on my part," he said raising his hands as he stepped back from the rail.

"I'm sorry too," I said with a sigh. "It's just been a very long few days. I'll give it some thought and talk to you about it later."

"Fair enough stay safe," he said as he stepped back through the door.

I got down stairs where Drake, Tom and Chris were already at the car talking to Roy and his men. I joined them and waited for a break in the conversation.

"We ready?" I asked curtly.

"Yeah we're good to go," Drake said.

"Good," I said as I walked over and held the seat forward so Chris could get in the back before I got in and closed the door.

Drake gave me a look and shrugged as he got in. When he saw that I wasn't going to take the bait he drove off with Roy behind us. We made it almost halfway home before he couldn't take not knowing anymore.

"You okay?" he asked.

"Yep I'm just ducky," I said.

"Okay, are you pissed at one of us or someone else?" Tom asked.

"I'll just be glad when this shit is all over," I said staring out my window at the ruins of deserted buildings we were passing by.

"Ah, it was someone inside!" Chris exclaimed from the back seat.

"What happened?" Drake inquired.

"Now they want me to be some kind of general or something," I said waving my hand dismissively.

"Well that makes perfect sense then. I'd be pissed too if someone wanted me to be in charge of something that I kind of started anyway," Tom said dripping sarcasm.

"Yeah hon, you lost me. This pissed you off why?" Chris asked.

"Because I'm not a fucking general, and this isn't a goddamned army! We're just a bunch of fucking morons running around with guns, getting ourselves killed that's why! Make a bit more fucking sense now?" I yelled.

"Dude, I get it. They probably could have picked a better time to bring it up," Drake said.

"He's right, you are the logical choice. Would you rather they put someone else in charge of our clan?" Chris asked knowing the answer.

"No, what I want is to lock down our border and stay the fuck out of this to keep the rest of my clan alive!" I said.

"You know that can't happen now, besides didn't you essentially start this fight when you told the colonel to go fuck himself? You think you can back out now?" Tom asked.

"Listen, I know you're feeling shitty about AJ and the others but you can't just give up because one person decided to not listen," Drake said.

"Yeah, and it was Liam, you knew he was gonna be trouble. You need to stop beating yourself up and come to terms with the fact that sometimes soldiers die. There's nothing you can do about it honey. I'm sorry to put it so bluntly but you know we're right," she said as she leaned forward between the seats.

"You know it wasn't your fault, we all know it, including AJ," Drake said quietly.

"I know," I said staring out the side window.

Chris leaned in and gave me a kiss on the cheek before sitting back. Drake drove on as I sat silently, trying to digest all that they had said. We got back into Menotomy shortly and went straight to the cemetery with Roy still behind us. We drove through the wrought iron entrance and down a small paved road to the back of the old burial ground.

"Thank you, all of you. You're right, sorry for freaking out," I said.

"It's why you keep us around, well that and the really good sex, at least that's why you keep me," Chris said with a sly grin.

"You aren't the only one that's good in bed," Drake said over his shoulder as he got out.

"Oh, I've heard all about you, from a whole lot of different girls ya whore," she said smiling.

"Just tryin' to keep our species alive is all," he said with a wink.

"One vagina at a time," Chris added.

"Hmm no, there's been more than a few times that there wasn't JUST one," he said with a smirk.

"Niiiice," I said as I closed the car door.

She walked over and slugged Drake in the arm. He responded immediately by tossing her up over his shoulder in a fireman carry and jogged toward Roy's truck. Chris was bellowing all the way to be put down. I smiled as I watched, they acted like siblings and it was good to see them have a little bit of fun, at least someone was.

A couple of Roy's team grabbed some shovels out of the equipment shed and we got to work digging. It took us a good three hours to get all three graves dug. We were all filthy when it came time to inter our friends. Roy and I said a few words of remembrance before they were laid to rest.

The hospital seemed like a ghost town compared to the chaos of Cambridge. The team leaders had let their men go home for a bit before heading back to MT. Auburn later this afternoon. We ran into Sam almost as soon as we got there and she wrapped her arms around Drake's neck covering his face in kisses. She thanked me for making sure he got home safely. I knew she was trying to say something sweet but considering how many didn't make it home it didn't help. I told her that of course he had to come home okay, who would I torment if he wasn't around? Everyone had a good chuckle and she dragged him off to their room so she could spend some time with him before we had to leave again.

Roy and Tom excused themselves to go wash up. Chris said she'd grab us something to eat from the kitchen and meet me in the room in a bit. I nodded numbly and wandered down the hall of the first floor away from them. I was distracted and needed to tend to that before I could think clearly.

I made my way up to the second floor and halfway down the long corridor of empty rooms. The room I was looking for was closed so I rapped hard on the heavy wooden door. Anne opened it after a few seconds. I stepped in and closed the door behind me.

"I knew it'd be you," she said as she crossed her arms.

"I bet you did," I said coldly.

Liam was staring out the window at the far end of the room. He hadn't reacted at all when I had come in. He was only wearing black cargo pants hanging low on his waist. His long hair hung down untied. His massive tattoo and scar covered shoulders were hunched as he stood stark still with one hand braced on the edge of the window frame.

"You know he feels awful," she said quietly.

"You know he fuckin' should," I spat back.

"I do, it was an accident Mack, he didn't mean it," she said.

"Don't you dare try and defend his fucking actions, you weren't there! He knew he was to stay put and follow orders, yet he didn't! Accident my ass, this is why we retired him years ago!" I said waving a finger in her face. "He's always been more dangerous to us than them!"

"I'm right here," Liam said from the far end of the room.

"You shut the fuck up! I'll let you know when I wanna talk to you!" I said angrier than I should have.

He was on me before I could blink, goddamn was he fast. He grabbed me by the shirt and raised me off the ground pinning me to the wall so that we were face to face, his lips curled back in a snarl that seemed a bit too much like a smile.

"Care to rephrase that?" he asked in a whisper.

"LIAM NOOO!" Anne screamed.

"Nope I think I'll stand by what I said," I said with a grin as I shifted my eyes up to his left. He glanced up to see that I had the barrel of my Sig dug into the side of his skull.

"Wanna put me down or does this end here?" I asked.

He grunted and lowered me to the ground as Anne swore and paced around the room ranting about how Liam needs to just think before he does things or some such nonsense. He turned and trudged back to the window, "I really am sorry Mack," he said as he sat on the ledge.

"I know you are," I said.

"I just didn't think that he would do that. I didn't ask him too." He said with a shrug.

"That's why you're dangerous; you don't understand working as a team. If any other of my team had jumped up in the middle of a battle all of us would have laid down cover fire. The only reason you didn't get my whole fucking team killed is that we didn't hear or see you until you had already moved," I jabbed him in the chest with a finger.

"I know," he started to say.

"NO, YOU OBVIOUSLY DON'T KNOW! IF YOU DID AJ WOULDN'T BE IN THE FUCKIN'GROUND RIGHT NOW, SO NO, YOU DON'T KNOW!" I screamed.

"Mack, please," Anne pleaded.

"You're right," Liam said staring down at his feet.

"When we head out, you work alone or with one other person. That person will have to volunteer to work with you because I'm sure as shit done signing death warrants. Are we clear?" I asked as I spun and stalked back toward the door.

"Yes sir," Liam said.

"Mack, no, just leave him here," Anne said.

"No, we need him. He wanted to go so this is how it's gonna be," I said with a shrug.

"You're gonna get him killed," she yelled.

"Better him than the rest of us," I said as I opened the door and stepped out into the hallway.

"FUCK YOU MACK!" she screamed from behind the heavy wooden door.

I was fifteen feet from the room before I heard the door open, "Stop, Mack cut the shit!" she demanded as she walked quickly toward me.

"What would you prefer I do? I wasn't kidding when I said I needed him. That's why I asked if he was good to go days ago," I said as I leaned against the wall.

"I'm not going to let you just send my husband to his death! You know how shitty he feels right now he'd walk into hell to make up for what he did," she said.

"That's exactly what I'm counting on actually," I said with a shrug.

She slapped me hard across the face just before she screamed that I was a heartless prick as loud as she could. She wound up to slap me again and I grabbed her by the wrist.

"Listen!" I said to get her attention.

"Let go of me you fuck!" she said yanking her hand out of my grasp.

"I have no intention of getting Liam killed," I said as I went back to leaning.

"What?" she asked.

"I just need him to follow orders and right now I've guaranteed that he will. He'll be fine, I will have him working alone or with one person but he should be okay, as okay as any of us will be. I was never just going to send him into a fiery screaming death, even if I was I'd still want him to be useful doing it," I said with a smirk.

"You promise this isn't just some way to get payback for AJ?" she asked.

"I promise. I wouldn't do that to you. After yesterday I'd do it to him, but not you," I said as I gave her a hug.

"Okay, I'm sorry I slapped you," she said.

"Its fine, been happening a lot lately," I said.

"Tell him we'll be leaving in two hours," I said as I turned.

"Will do, I know I don't have to say this but please be careful," she said behind me.

"What fun would that be?" I said and gave a small smile.

I made my way up to the third floor and found Chris relaxing in a chair, dressed in what looked like only a long black t shirt. Her feet up on the window ledge and she was working on a bowl of some kind of soup. She heard me walk in and said hello over her shoulder just before I heard a slurping sound followed a satisfied "AHHH".

"I love soup!" she said sounding like a kid.

"Is it good?" I asked walking up behind her and kissing the top of her still damp head.

"If you like warm dish water posing as vegetable soup then yeah it's awesome!" she said with a giggle.

"Great." I said flatly.

"How'd it go with wherever you went?" she asked while putting the bowl down on a side table.

"Good I guess, I went to go see Anne and Liam," I said as I made my way into the bathroom where she had left a basinet of clean water, soap, a washrag and a towel.

"Doesn't sound so good from your tone," she said from the other room.

"Sorry honey, I'm just distracted," I said as pulled off my shirt and washed up.

"It's been a long few days," she said.

"I don't think it's gonna get any better soon," I said.

I finished toweling off my face and saw in the grimy mirror over the sink that she was standing in the doorway behind me. I tossed the towel to the side and turned to see her leaning against the door frame.

"Guess we need to take a few minutes to enjoy being alone then," she said stepping into me and wrapping her arms around my waist and burying her face in my chest.

"I told them we'd be leaving in a couple hours," I said as I smelled her hair.

"Guess you should work fast then hmm?" she asked as she grinned up at me and took my hand leading me toward the bed.

"With the mood I'm in that may not be a problem," I said smiling.

"Feeling nasty are we?" she asked as she stopped in front of the large window and pulled my arms around her. "I do so love a quickie."

I kissed her neck softly and slid my hands up under the edges of her t-shirt, "Had a bit of an adrenaline rush when I was dealing with Liam so I'm kinda…" I felt the string of her

148

panties riding high up on her hips as I slid my hands around and up the front of her shirt cupping one perky small breast in my callused hand.

"Worked up already?" she half moaned.

"You could say that," I said as I tugged softly on her nipple while my free hand slid inside the front of her panties.

She moaned softly as I played with her and she ground her ass firmly up against my crotch, "Yeah you are," she said softly as I felt her press back harder against me.

I kissed her ear softly and slowly worked my way down the right side of her neck. I switched to her other nipple so it didn't feel neglected and gave it a gentle tug. She leaned so that the back of her head rested on the top of my chest as she continued to grind her hips against me. I slid her shirt up the rest of the way and let it rest on top of her pert breasts. I worked my hand up and held her gently by the neck cupping the bottom of her jaw.

She cooed softly and squirmed as I could feel her getting more wet the quicker I played with her clit. She liked having little circles traced around the edge of it before lightly flicking it back and forth. Her tiny hand slid between us, ran up and down the length of my shaft. She hooked her fingers in the waistband of my cargo pants and pulled me tight against her.

I pulled her head back taut and leaned down to kiss her soft parted lips hard. Her tongue searched for mine as she moaned softly into my mouth as I flicked her clit. The kiss was long and passionate. She pulled away when we were both near breathless. Her eyes were shut tight as she reached behind me, dug her nails into my hip as I felt her body begin to tighten up. She moaned loudly, then took a breath and seemed to hold it as her legs started to shake. She gasped and grabbed me with her other hand to keep her balance as I strummed her clit faster. She moaned one last time and bit down hard on her bottom lip as her body finally relaxed. Her eyes still squeezed shut as she tried to catch her breath.

Breathing heavy and still having the back of her head resting on my chest she hooked her thumbs in the waistband of her panties and slid them down to her knees, quickly wiggling them to the floor as I unbuttoned and unzipped my pants. She leaned forward against the thick cool glass of the window and I took her by her round, supple hips and slid myself deep inside her. She moaned as I entered her and pressed her hands flat against the glass so she could push herself back against me driving me deeper still.

I tilted my head back and closed my eyes enjoying how warm, wet and tight she felt. She always seemed to feel like the perfect fit. I looked down and watched as she slowly ground her ass up against me. I smiled at the curve of her tiny little frame, up to her head that was hung between her shoulders as she worked her hips.

She must have felt me staring at her because she glanced over her shoulder with a knowing grin, "You gonna fuck me or am I gonna do all the work today?" she asked before she giggled.

I smirked as I slid my left hand over the dimple on her ass and up the curve of her arched back until it came to rest on her shoulder. My fingers dug deep into the muscle of her shoulder as well as the soft flesh on her hip and I drove deep into her. She yelped and smiled before hanging her head again, "That's what I was looking for," she said to no one.

Her legs spread slightly and she slid one hand down the glass bracing herself on the ledge of the window. Her tits and left cheek were firmly pressed against the window. I let her hips set the rhythm as I pumped to match her. I could feel her reaching her climax again. She started to contract around my cock, squeezing it tight, as I continued to thrust deep inside her. Picking up the pace I slapped her ass hard before sliding my hand that was on her hip up to join the other on her shoulders and pulled her away from the window as I pounded away at her now sopping wet pussy. Her breathing was heavy and the moans louder as she started to tense up. She forced herself against the window again as her climax rocked her and I felt her legs quiver as every muscle tensed up. She let out an almost scream as she came hard for me this time and shoved her ass up against me squirming it in circles on my cock, the walls of her pussy quickly squeezing and releasing me over and over again.

"Oh god, don't stop!" she yelled as she continued her orgasm.

I drove myself furiously into her, panting as I could hear the wet slap of our sweaty bodies slamming against each other.

She came again almost instantly and reached back clawing at my hips as I pounded into her from behind. I couldn't take much more and then I felt her walls squeeze me tight again even faster than before. I exploded inside her as she moaned loud and slapped her hand off the thick plate glass. She shoved herself back onto me, her pace slowing, finally. I could hear her ragged breathing and see the steam of it on the window as I leaned forward and rested my head on the back of her shoulder. I kissed her neck softly.

She turned her head just far enough that I felt her lips kissing mine. I could taste her salty, sweet sweat as I kissed her and she purred before pulling away. She turned around to lean against the ledge that she had been bracing herself on for the last few minutes. She pulled me to her by the waist of my pants as she kissed my sweaty chest and my stubble covered chin. I looked down at her and she smiled up at me in return. We kissed for awhile as I wrapped my arms around her and she snuggled into me. There were more than a couple "I love you s" from both parties.

Chapter 17

The street in front of Mt. Auburn was littered with vehicles by the time we got back. It was dark out now and Drake pulled up in front of the main entrance. The four of us got out of the car and headed inside. Roy had taken Liam with him to pick up his team and would be here in a little while. Anne had wanted to come with us but changed her mind when I told her that Sam was staying behind as well. I also left Lily with her. Lily hated loud noises and if they began shelling again she'd just be terrified.

George met us in the lobby with Gomez. Chris told me that she was going to head down to check on patients before she gave me a quick kiss and disappeared down the stairs. George led me and Drake upstairs to his temporary command center and sat us down. Tom had decided to find a bit of shuteye and told us he'd meet us later.

"Mack, we have a problem," George said.

"Do you have any idea how tired I am of hearing that?" I asked him.

"What's wrong you can't find your Buffy DVD?" Drake asked.

"No, that's in his little blue duffel bag that he keeps the DVD player and his porn in," Gomez chuckled.

"Are you assholes done?" George asked.

"I suppose your face is red enough now, yeah we're done," Drake said smirking.

"Great, thanks, Hags says he can't get here because the colonel has set up a perimeter along the Charles. He's got checkpoints and roaming patrols covering every way in or out. I got in touch with Keith on this side of the bridge and he confirms that it's now shut down as well," George said and the plopped himself down in a chair.

"Okay," I said as I spun slowly in the black leather office chair, "This can work too. If he can't get to us, and if they haven't forcefully disarmed him yet, then they probably don't know that we are working with him. As long as that remains true, then we can just let him and his men know when we are ready to go. That way they can hit them from behind and work their way across to rendezvous with us," I said nodding slowly to myself while the chair spun.

"I'll let him know and tell him that he may want to rally his men somewhere away from those patrols," George said making a note.

"Yeah, good call, that the only problem right now?" I asked.

"I'd say that was enough," George answered.

"True, I'm gonna go downstairs to see who's all here and let them know this little piece of good news. George I need you and whatever team leaders are here with me for this," I said.

"Sure thing, why?" he asked, as he picked up the radio and gave a quick call for the guys to meet us on the first floor.

"Cuz I need you to start working on strategy and troop deployment along with any other little details you can think of so you can start putting it together with Brett," I said.

"I thought that was your job," he said.

"Not this time, me and what's left of Alpha are gonna be busy when this shit storm hits," I said as I made my way to the door.

"Doing what?" George asked from behind me.

"We're gonna be hunting the colonel, to make sure he doesn't bother us again," I said walking down the cement stairwell.

"When were you planning on telling me this?" he asked sounding annoyed.

"Right about now," I quipped.

"You're an asshole," he said.

"And then some," I replied.

By the time we got to the main floor George had almost finished grumbling to himself about being left out of the loop. Gomez was already with us and Buck. Jay, Teddy and Cain were waiting in the lobby. Drake wasn't a team leader but he was my second and he'd have tagged along anyway even if he wasn't. I asked one of the guards at the door if he knew where his boss was and he told me that Matt along with some of the other clan heads were in a conference room at the end of the hall.

I swung open the heavy wooden door and found seven of the clan heads inside. Most of them were sitting while a couple paced. Among them were Matt, Brett, Mike and surprisingly Dani from Littleton. She had inherited her husband's title after he was killed at Fenway. They all stopped talking as we walked in and I grabbed a seat at the head of the table nearest the door.

"Good to see you all made it here safely," I said.

"We've all been comparing notes and sharing information for the last hour or so," Matt said.

"Well, I'll add what little I have then. Hags and his men can't seem to get here right now since it seems they've put up checkpoints and patrols all along the river," I said.

"But we needed his people," Mike said.

"We still do, it can be worked out, I'm not too worried. Which leads me to my next point," I put my palm out flat and motioned toward George," This is George, he's ex-military, as well as my command and control guy. He's very good with logistics, planning and an all around nice guy."

"Umm, hi all," George said with a small wave.

"George is going to be working with Brett on planning our troop movements and all kinds of logistical fun. He will also be working with Hags to coordinate that end of things as well," I said.

"I think we just assumed that you would be taking care of that," Dani said looking around the room at the other confused clan heads, all except Brett and Matt.

"George has my complete and utter faith. He will also be working with some of our other team leaders. I may be the clan chief but George is usually who I turn to when we work out a plan for an operation," I said.

"Won't you be helping to plan this and leading the men?" Art, the clan chief of the ABC's asked.

"Not at first no, my team and I have our own op to plan and run," I said vaguely.

"Excuse me?" Dani asked starting to sound peeved.

"Okay, listen," I said as I stood, "I am constantly in contact with my men. Nothing is going to happen without me knowing about it, even if I wanted it too. I just can't do everything myself. My people have gotten by all these years by working together as a team. All I was trying to tell you was that George is your "go to" guy when it comes to planning and logistics. If I need to know something I'm sure that he'll tell me."

"We've been pretty secluded the last few years so I have no idea how your clans run, but we found that a chain of command works best for our people," George said as he stepped forward to grab people's attention. "We have Mack here and then we have Drake as his second. I fall into the chain by making sure everyone stays in contact. After that we have team leaders and patrol leaders and so forth. It's worked well for us so far and this is not new to us it's just on a much larger scale."

"That's all well and good but what are you going to be doing while all this planning is going on?" Dani asked calmly.

"He's going to hunt down and kill the colonel," Brett said somberly.

"Not how I would have put that," I heard Drake mumble to himself as I scanned the room to see the shocked expressions of the clan chiefs that didn't know.

"No shit huh?" I whispered knowing he could hear me.

"Is this true?" Art asked raising an eyebrow in my direction.

"That's the plan," I answered.

"Good," Dani said from the other end of the table.

"I think I'm in love," I heard Roy whisper behind me.

"How is that going to solve our problem?" Mike asked.

"According to what the colonel told me himself, he was brought here to get us under control any way possible. He rounded us all up and tried to kill us. If we hadn't escaped, we'd all have been replaced with people more agreeable. He OK'd the kidnapping of doctors as well as my wife and set an ambush where I lost valuable men just a few weeks ago. So far, all of this seems to be stemming from him. The way I see it, we get rid of him and everything else goes back to the way it was before he got here," I said with a shrug.

"Won't his second just take over?" Art asked.

"From what I can tell, the colonel was brought here specifically because he is their "Fixer", you know, the guy they bring in to take care of trouble. Chances are that his second isn't as dedicated," I said.

"At the very least, the troops have to wait for them to assign a new commanding officer from out west and we send them a strong message that we will not just lie down. At the most, we rout them and push them out for good. Then we all get to go back to living our happy little lives," George said leaning on the table.

"I dunno if I can condone outright murder," Art said.

"Murder?" Dani said pushing her chair back as she slapped the table and stood, "This man **MURDERED** our people including my husband! He would have murdered you all if it hadn't been for Duncan and the others. The only thing I regret is that I won't be there to pull the trigger! How is this even a question?"

"Please Dani, calm down," Matt said. "I think some of us may just have a problem with the idea of assassinating someone. It sets a difficult precedent."

"It doesn't set any precedent at all!" Dani yelled. "I don't recall him asking any of us for permission or help. The man is offering to save all of the clans not just his own and all you seem to care about is your conscious!"

"She is awesome, can we keep her?" I heard Teddy whisper in my ear.

"Danielle, please calm down and have a seat," Brett said quietly.

"I'm not done yet sir," she said, steel in her voice. "Mr. Mackenzie," she paused waiting for me to catch her eyes. "I fully support your plan and trust you implicitly to rectify our predicament. If I or my clan can assist you in any way, all you need do is ask. As for those of you that have a problem with Mr. Mackenzie's plan I strongly suggest you grow up. This is war gentlemen. Fight to win or don't fight at all. There is no middle ground," she nodded, smiled to herself and sat down quietly.

I heard applause from behind me and let slip a small sigh as I glanced back to see that every one of my guys had busted out a slow clap for their new heroine. "Thank you Dani, well said and I greatly appreciate the support," I said as I spun back around.

"Is there any other business?" I asked, glancing around the room, waiting. They all sat there like chastised little boys, staring at the table or the tops of their shoes, anywhere except at me or Dani.

"Alright then," I said as I stood, "I will leave George and Gomez here with you all to start figuring things out while I go take care of other things."

Roy, Drake and the others followed me out into the hallway. By the time we were back in the lobby they were all talking about how well Dani had put the others in their place. They suddenly went quiet when they heard her voice come from behind us calling for me to wait for her. The others continued on by me and Drake slapped me on the shoulder, chuckling as he headed toward the stairwell.

"Nice work in there," I said folding my arms across my chest.

"Thanks," she said with a smile, "I used to be a trial lawyer."

"That makes sense," I said with a grin.

She was a small girl, about the same height as Chris. She was more petite and less curvy than her though. She had olive skin, big, dark brown eyes and shoulder length dark brown hair. I was guessing Italian, but she could have been anything I suppose. She was wearing a black wool pea coat a red checked flannel unbuttoned, with a black tank top beneath it and faded black jeans tucked into knee-high black leather boots.

"Was there something you needed?" I asked.

"I was mainly trying to find a reason to get out of that room. I figure I can walk with you for a little bit, then head over and spend some time with my men," she said as we began walking away from the conference room.

"Do you really think your plan will work?" she asked.

"I'm still working on a plan but yeah I do and if we do it right it will save a bunch of lives on both sides hopefully," I said with a shrug.

"Do you know how you're going to get in town since they have everything cordoned off?" she asked leaning against the railing in the stairwell.

"Nope, not yet, like I said, still working on a plan," I grinned.

"What are you smiling at?" she asked with a slight tilt of her head.

"You just seem to have a lot of questions is all," I said trying to not sound paranoid, which I was.

"You don't trust me?" she said as she batted her lashes at me mockingly.

"I don't trust much of anyone anymore," I said.

"Good," she said suddenly becoming very stern again. "I see you being a good leader for this group and working hard to keep us all safe and alive, I'd have been disappointed if you weren't suspicious," she grinned and winked up at me.

"A test huh?" I said as I leaned against the concrete wall across from her.

"Yeah, don't worry though, you passed this one with flying colors." she stepped toward me and smiled, "and since you have, I'll just say this, if there's anything at all I can do to help, please just let me know."

"Just make sure they stay on track in their planning. I do trust George, but the way you manhandled them today I think he could use your help with keeping them in line," I said.

"I'm really good at manhandling things," she said with a smirk, "I'm off to visit my men, then I'll come back to help George. G'night," she said as she disappeared through the door that led back into the lobby leaving me alone to wonder whether she was flirting with me or not. After almost a minute I decided I didn't care and just enjoyed it as I walked down to the ER to check on Chris.

I found her at the nurses' station going over charts with a couple of the docs from our clinic. I waited patiently leaning against the old wooden counter that circled the station. Chris made her way over to me when she had finished, stretched and leaned in to give me a kiss. She stopped just short of my lips and pulled back with a scrunched up face. "Why are you all smiley? I thought you were dealing with the clan chiefs."

"I was and I'm not all… smiley," I said dismissively and leaned in to give her a quick peck.

"You are too all smiley. What'd you do?" she asked raising an eyebrow at me.

"I think someone just flirted with me a little is all," I said with a shrug.

"Nice! Was it one of the nurses?" she asked.

"No."

"Doctors?"

"No."

"Is George hitting the bottle and calling you Rosalita again?" she asked and giggled.

"No," I said. "I really need to find out who that Rosalita chick is."

"So who was it then?" she asked.

"It was another clan chief," I said scratching the back of my neck.

"Oh, we have a female clan head?" she asked.

"Yeah, she took over for her husband. They got him at Fenway," I said.

"Wow that sucks," she paused, "Is she cute?"

"Yeah, not bad," I answered.

"Nice, I'll have to meet her sometime,"

"Aren't you the least bit jealous?" I asked.

"Oh honey, no, I'm not jealous," she laughed, "I've been married to you long enough to know you're not going anywhere."

"True," I said nodding.

"I'm off to do some rounds. I'll meet you in our room later on. Make sure your new friend is gone by then," she said with a wink, a pat on the ass and then she was gone.

"Cute," I mumbled to myself as I walked off.

Chapter 18

"There is no way into Boston from here," Tom said throwing his hands up in frustration.

"There has to be, we just have to figure it out," I said as I paced the room.

We had been cooped up for over an hour now trying to work out our plan to assassinate the colonel. So far we hadn't even come up with how to get into Boston. Tom, Teddy, Drake, Roy and I had spent the first half hour discussing what gear to bring. The last half hour had been nothing but wracking our brains on how to get there.

"Okay, why don't we grab one of the duck tour things and go across the Charles that way. They're amphibious," Teddy said.

"Cuz the duck tour buses are ON the other side of the Charles. If we could get there to take one we wouldn't need it. Besides, do you have any idea how loud those things are?" Drake explained.

"Are we sure we can't just walk across the river?" Roy asked.

"No we aren't sure, but do we really wanna take that chance and have one, or all of us fall into a freezing river that's being patrolled by armed men that want to kill us?" I asked.

"Probably not," Roy answered before he let out a massive sigh.

"I still like the 93 idea," Teddy said with a shrug.

"And I'm telling you 93 collapsed, the bridge and overpass are gone Teddy, gone do you get that?" Drake said sounding pissed.

"Right, that's where the rope bridge comes in…" Teddy tried to say.

"It's like three-quarters of a fucking mile Ted. How're you planning on building this rope bridge, did you grow fucking wings?" Drake snapped.

"It's not that long," Teddy said dismissively.

"When did we become the A-Team Murdock?" Tom asked glancing over at Teddy

"Okay, maybe it isn't that long a span Teddy but we still don't have time to build a rope bridge," I said rubbing the bridge of my nose between my thumb and forefinger.

"But if we took a compound bow and shot it…" Teddy started.

"I SAID NO TEDDY, FOR FUCK'S SAKE!" I yelled as I pounded the table.

"This fucker just doesn't get it," Drake said.

"Enough," Roy said.

"Can we go through the train tunnels?" Tom asked.

"Not from here, the red line goes above ground to get over the river," I said.

There were plenty of tunnels in Cambridge and Boston. Both cities were old. I'm sure they both had an overabundance of abandoned tunnels and access ways. Most though went above ground when it came to the river, at least all the ones we knew of.

"There are lines that go other places though," Tom said rubbing his scruff covered chin.

"What're you thinking?" I asked.

"Well, the red line goes above ground as does the green line over by Lechmere. We'd have to check but there is the orange, blue, and silver lines that could get us there," Tom said.

"The orange line goes over land to Boston too, that I know. The other two I have no idea," Drake said.

"The Blue line goes underground into Boston," Teddy said.

"You took the blue line a lot did you?" Drake asked.

"Yeah, actually I did. I used to date this chick from Revere and we would take the T in when we would go in town from her house," Teddy said.

"It goes underground across the river?" I asked.

"No, it goes under the harbor. I think it's in the same line with the Callahan and Sumner," he said,

"Well that could be really helpful," I said happily.

"What are the chances that the section that goes under Boston harbor is still intact?" Roy asked.

"I have no idea but if it was built when the other tunnels were I trust it a lot more than anything built during the big dig," I said.

"True," Roy agreed.

"I guess we should probably start there then," I said.

"What if we get there and it's flooded," Roy asked.

"Hopefully one of the other two isn't I guess," I shrugged.

We spent the next couple of hours going over timelines, gear and our route once we were out of the tunnels. We decided to take a break and go see what supplies we could scavenge here at Mt. Auburn. We were pretty sure we'd have to stop by the shop on our way to the tunnel anyway but figured it wouldn't hurt to start looking here first. Drake waited until everyone else left the room before he stood and closed the door and leaned against it.

"You feel good about this plan?" he asked.

"As good as I do any of our plans," I said with a shrug. "Why?"

"I dunno, I have a really bad feeling about this one," he said as he paced the front of the room.

"It's not perfect..." I started to say.

"Not only is it not perfect but we have no idea what's out there. None of us have been up in that area in at least four and a half years. How do we even know it's still there?" he asked throwing his arms up in the air as he paced.

"You're right but you heard how limited our options were," I said.

"Shouldn't we take a day and go check it out? I mean if we had more time..." he said thinking out loud.

"There is no more time. We need to go soon and hope we find a way across. The colonel isn't going to wait until we're sure we have a secret back door," I said leaning back in my chair.

"I know. I'm just letting you know up front that I have a very bad feeling about this one," he said as he plopped himself down in his chair.

"Noted," I said. "We'll be as careful as we can. You know that, we always are. That's the best I can give you for now," I said as I stood.

"Hope it's enough," he said quietly.

We made our way down to the conference room where George had been meeting with the clan chiefs trying to figure out logistics and strategies. When we got there he and Arthur were the only ones left in the room. They were sitting across from each other studying a map they had laid of the Boston/Cambridge area. Finally, George glanced up at us, his elbow on the table and his chin resting on his palm as he asked, "How'd it go?"

"We're gonna go in via the blue line," I answered as I sat down and looked over the maps.

"Interesting idea, are we sure the tunnel is open?" he asked moving the Boston map around so he could check out the blue line route better.

"Nope," Drake answered.

"Heh, even more interesting then," he said.

"He's got a bad feeling about the whole thing," I said as I hooked a thumb toward Drake.

"He should, so far from what I've heard, it sucks," George said as he shrugged at me with a grin.

"It does but we've come to the conclusion that it seems to be the only way in at the moment," I said.

"Oh, that's quite possible as well but it still sucks," George agreed.

"Anyway, I sent the guys off to scrounge us some equipment, the rest we'll have to grab from the shop. How's it going here? You've lost some people I see," I said.

"Art here has been very helpful, he's ex-military as well so they sort of gave him the job of working with me to help figure everything out," George said.

"I tried to tell them I was just a mechanic but they didn't seem to care," Art said.

"Of course they didn't, they wanted to be able to dish it all off on someone and you gave them the perfect reason," Drake said.

"Yeah, I probably should have kept my mouth shut," he said scratching his head.

"Well, I for one am very happy you didn't, God knows I could use the help, these two are useless," George said with a wink.

"How's your timeline comin'?" I asked.

"Good, we figure we should be ready in less than two days, if we have that long," George said.

"Okay we can do two days as well. That should give us plenty of time to get in position," I replied.

"You're gonna use our attacking them as a distraction to get the colonel?" Art asked.

"Kind of, we're gonna use your attack to draw most of them away from Fenway so we can GET to the colonel," I answered.

"Hmm, that makes sense," he said with a slow nod.

"Two days it is then!" George exclaimed. "You better be on time."

Chapter 19

We left Mt. Auburn early the next morning. Chris was not happy with me to say the least. She did agree with what we were trying to do, she just didn't want us doing it. I understood how she felt, she was afraid none of us were going to come back and that was definitely a possibility. It took a while but we talked it through enough that by the time we fell asleep she was okay with the idea. This by no means meant she **LIKED** the idea.

We loaded what gear we could find into Roy's pickup, checked in with George, Art, and the clan heads before we piled into the beat up black Ford pickup. I sat in the open bed with Drake, Liam, and Tom watching the hospital retreat into the distance as we drove off. The window to the cab was open behind me and I could hear Teddy prattling on about something to Roy. I smiled as I wondered how long one of the most patient men I had ever met would last.

"He just never stops does he?" Drake asked beside me.

"Nope," I said with a grin.

"Even money says we don't make it back to the shop before Roy pulls over and makes one of us get up front," Tom said as he sat on the wheel well.

"Or he'll just punch Teddy," Drake said.

"Nah, Roy's too nice a guy. I think he'd pull over first," Tom said nodding to himself.

"He's a better man than I then, I'd just punch him," Drake said with a shrug.

"Wouldn't it be easier if I just shot him?" I heard Roy yell from the driver's seat.

"You'd get too much blood on your upholstery," Liam chimed in seriously.

"Too true my friend," Roy said chuckling. "Teddy doesn't bother me. Sometimes, when he's going on and on it brings me back before all this. So, in a way it's kinda nice actually,"

"HAH! See Roy likes talkin' to me," Teddy said proudly, sticking his head out the back window of the cab.

"No one else does, so shut up and turn around," Drake said with a grin as he flicked Teddy's left ear.

Drake and I went through the pile of backpacks at our feet rechecking our supplies as we drove down Alewife Brook parkway so that we could cut through Belmont to get us back to the shop. We hadn't found a lot besides weapons, ammo and food at Mt. Auburn. We had lanterns, flashlights, and rechargeable batteries at the shop. I was unconscious at the time but as far as George told me the military had just secured me then headed out with their wounded and dead. They hadn't seemed to care about anything of use we may have had at the shop.

I noticed that spring was coming as we drove quietly along the streets of what used to be an affluent suburb of Boston. The temperature had warmed up maybe ten degrees or so in the last couple weeks and some of the snow had melted. There were actual spots on the street now where you could see pavement. It was by no means warm but it was at least tolerable, almost nice, during the day.

It took us about twenty minutes to make our way to the shop. The heavy steel plate gate was still open from the attack. Roy pulled up slowly and nudged it fully open with the front bumper of the truck. He made his way down the narrow driveway and parked in the back near the door. Teddy volunteered to go close the gate as the rest of us hopped out of

171

the truck and made our way down the old wooden stairs. The door had been blown off the hinges when the troops had busted in to get me.

I hadn't considered how odd it would be to come back here. It had been home for a long time now, but I hadn't seen it since the day they dragged me out of here unconscious. I touched the scorch marks on the brick wall where they had placed the charges to take out the hinges of our door. I saw Tom picking up George's command chair as I got to the bottom of the stairs. Drake was standing in the kitchen with his hands on his hips taking in the destruction that the initial firefight had caused.

"That's it, we are **NOT** having people over anymore," he said as he glanced over his shoulder at me.

"Yep, no more parties for us," I agreed.

"They fucked this place up," he said as he shook his head.

I chuckled and patted him on the shoulder as I walked out and down the hallway toward my office. There was dirt, dust, shell casings, blown out wallboard and ceiling tiles covering the floor as I made my way down the long hallway that we had fought in. It seemed like forever ago but it had only been about a week. George had sent a team to bring the dead home but not to clean anything up. Things had been at such a hellish pace since the attack that I hadn't even asked how many we had lost that day. I suppose it was possible that we only had wounded but I felt horrible having not asked.

I swung open the door to my office and saw that it seemed to be exactly as I had left it. I guess that was one of the benefits of having your office tucked back out of the way. I grabbed the Maglite and bottle of Maker's Mark out of my desk. I turned the Maglite on to test it then tested the Maker's Mark as well. Both seemed to work just fine. I tucked them into my pack along with a spare knife and a couple of clips for my Sig that were sitting at the bottom of the drawer. I took a long look around and slowly closed the door behind me, wondering if I was ever going to see this room again.

I got to the stairs and was about to make my way up to the armory when I got a strong urge to stay on this floor for a couple more minutes. I strolled along the corridor until I got to the spot where I had dropped the behemoth of a soldier that had almost killed me. His body was gone, just as I knew it would be, but the blood was still there. From the look of it he had bled out almost where I had left him. There were drag marks that let me know he had made it a few feet before he died. Good for him, fucker had almost killed me with his bare hands.

I heard voices from upstairs as I made my way to the armory and stopped to listen. I could have sworn I heard a female voice. I pulled out one of my pistols to be on the safe side. I got to the landing and came face to face with the mysterious voice. She was short, wearing a long wool jacket and a scarf around her head. She smiled as I turned to face her.

"Oh, hello there Mack!" she said.

"Hi there Mary," I said congenially as I holstered my pistol. Mary was one of the clan. She lived down the street from the shop. She was a sweet lady in her early to mid sixties who worked at the inside garden we had at the high school.

"I'm sorry I hope I didn't startle you," she said.

"Just being careful is all," I said smiling at her. "Is everything okay?"

"Yes, yes, I was just on my way to work when I saw your truck pull in. We were all so worried at the garden I thought I'd check on you. You aren't the only one that can take care of people around here," she said with a grin.

"Nice to know we were missed," I said as I leaned against the railing.

"We heard the fight but the troops were gone before any of us had shown up," she said.

"It's probably best that they were Mary, we don't want anyone to get hurt," I said.

"Except you boys," she said somberly.

"No, we don't **WANT** to get hurt, just comes with the job sometimes," I said before I shrugged.

"Someone told me the clinic was empty too?" she asked.

"Yes for the moment. You can find everyone up at the old hospital on the hill. Please do me a favor and let everyone know that if they need supplies or treatment they can go up there anytime just like down here," I said.

"Of course of course," she said. "Is that your new home base?"

"Only for now I hope, we may be back here as early as a few days, might be a couple weeks. As you can see the place is a mess," I grinned. "I think we may need to fire the cleaning staff."

"What happened?" she asked.

"They found out where we were and came to stop us, get us back under control, or try to." I said.

"Then how can you come back here? Why don't you just stay up at the hospital?" she asked sounding worried.

"We're right in the middle of making sure they don't come back to get us again," I said as I put a hand on her shoulder.

"For good?" she asked eyes wide.

"That's the plan," I answered.

"Oh, that would be very nice! I do so worry about you all sometimes," she said as she gave me a quick hug.

"Wow, I didn't know that. That's very sweet," I said as I returned the hug.

"We all worry about you. You've helped us so much. We're family, of course we worry," she said as she shook a finger at me.

"Thank you," I said almost blushing.

"I'm gonna go to work now, but I'll tell everyone there about the hospital and what's going on. Don't worry, we'll spread the word," she said as she stopped in the doorway. "You're on your way to fight them now aren't you?"

"Soon ma'am," I said.

"Stay safe and try to bring yourself and everyone else home alive, we need you," she said sounding sad.

"I'll do my best," I said.

"You always do, that's why we love you," she said before she waved and disappeared down the driveway toward the hole in the fence.

I was still smiling to myself when I got to the doorway to the armory. Drake was inside looking in the drawers for something. "I heard voices," he said still rummaging.

"Mary came by to check on us. What are you looking for?" I asked as I hopped up onto the counter.

"Just checking for more recharged batteries, seems George did a good job moving most of them up to the hospital.

There's enough here for our stuff. I just like to have lots of extras," he said as he sighed and gave up on that drawer.

"Maybe there's some in the store room," I said as he picked up his duffel bag and came toward the door.

"I think that's where Tom and Roy were checking. Teddy and Liam were checking the food stores and back up storage room," he said as we walked down the corridor that led to Tom and Roy.

A few minutes after we got there Teddy and Liam joined us in the store room. Liam was lugging a duffel bag stuffed with equipment while Teddy had something that was rolled up tucked under his arm.

"What ya got there Teddy?" Roy asked.

"I found us a tent." Teddy chirped.

"Teddy, we don't need a tent," Drake said.

"Shouldn't we bring it just in case?" Teddy asked.

"In case what? We get stuck in the woods and have to sing camp songs and roast marshmallows?" Drake asked sarcastically.

"Fine," he said as he dropped the tent where he stood.

"Does that mean we don't need the marshmallows now?" Liam asked as he reached into the duffel bag and pulled out an unopened bag.

"Yeah I guess so. They're probably stale anyway," Teddy said sounding depressed.

"Hhmph," Liam said as he dropped the bag and pulled out two more adding them to the pile.

"If we have everything on the list, can we go now?" I asked.

"Yes sir, I believe we are as set as we're gonna be," Roy said.

"Good let's get on with this then, I'm getting antsy," I said as we made our way outside to the truck.

We stopped by the hospital to see Sam, Anne and Lily. Tom's wife worked at the clinic so she was there as well. Roy and Teddy didn't have any close family so they just made sure they got a hot cup of coffee. Lily whined as I gave her a kiss on the head before we left. Anne and Sam both threatened me with a horrible, horrible demise if I didn't bring myself and their men home safely. There were many hugs and some tears as we all piled back into the truck. After the waving was done we drove quietly down Summer Street. The enormity of the situation struck me like a blow. This wasn't like our normal op. Those were always in town where we knew almost every inch and every trick. Where we were going was completely foreign and we may very well not be lucky enough to make it back home.

Great, NOW I get Drake's bad feeling.

Chapter 20

We were starting to lose the light by the time we got to Revere. For the first time since the Storm I got a glimpse of the Atlantic Ocean. The sky was grey and blended into the sea itself. What used to be the main strip that ran along the beach was now submerged beneath a few feet of water. I could still see the remnants of the seawall poking up here and there so I knew that it was only four or five feet out to that point. What I didn't know was if this was high tide or low tide.

The gazebos, bathroom huts and any of the other small buildings that used to dot the beach had fallen to massive decay or been swept out to sea. Many of the row of stores and restaurants that, at one time, sat safely across the street from the water were now flooded, listing to one side or had fallen down completely.

I used to look forward to the summers up here in New England so that I could go lie on the beach and swim in the ocean. I loved boats, fishing, anything that would get me to the coast. Now, standing in the bed of the pickup gazing out at the angry grey sea crashing onto the shore, I didn't like the idea of the ocean very much. She seemed vengeful now and I dreaded seeing what she had wrought on the rest of the coastline as we got closer to Boston.

Teddy led Roy to the old train station and we followed a road that ran parallel to it until we saw an opening so we could drive right onto the tracks themselves. We rumbled along slowly trying to be quiet until we lost the last of the afternoon light. I smelled fires somewhere but we saw no signs of them. A mile or so away from the station Roy parked the truck off to the side of the tracks behind some bushes and we hopped out to grab our gear.

"Why are we walking from here again?" Tom asked as he shouldered his backpack.

"A. Because I like my truck and don't want to snap an axle. B. Because it's a lot easier to be sneaky and quiet if you aren't driving a big truck. Oh, and C. because to be honest Tom you're getting a little chunky and I think the walk will do you good," Roy said with a grin.

"Wouldn't it be easier to get away though if we ran into something we couldn't deal with?" Tom asked.

"Like what?" Drake asked. "We have a few miles to go before we have to worry about running into troops."

"What, like big haired Revere chicks or some Guido with no shirt and a thick ass chain around his neck?" Teddy asked with a chuckle.

"Yes, we're all worried about no neck douche bags and big haired hookers Tom but I think we'll be okay without the truck," I said as I started down the tracks behind Drake who was on point.

"We'd be screwed if they were mutant hookers though," Drake said over his shoulder.

"What's their mutation, big hair or whiny voices?" Roy asked.

"They have the mutant ability to suck all the blood out of you through your dick," Liam said somberly from the back of the group.

"Damn! That just isn't a pleasant thought at all," Teddy commented.

"Wouldn't that make them vampires or zombies?" Tom asked.

"I thought zombies only wanted brains," Teddy said.

"You're safe then," Drake snickered.

"Zombies do want brains but that'd be how we get screwed… zombie hookers, they just keep coming," I said with a smirk.

"Oh dear god, that was awful!" Drake exclaimed.

"What?" Tom asked.

"Never mind," Roy said. "It obviously went over your head and Drake was right it was terrible."

As night fell we walked along with less conversation. It was a new place and we didn't know who was out there or whether they were friendly or not. Drake and I tried to stay mostly on the railroad ties but the rest of the team had abandoned that idea. We made quite a ruckus walking in the gravel that lined the tracks. Normally, it wouldn't be a problem but sound traveled a lot further now that there was very little ambient noise to drown it out.

We saw some fires here and there off in the distance but none of them were very close to the tracks we were on. We traveled without our flashlights mainly because we had no idea how much we would need them later and also to draw less attention to ourselves. We came to a tree that had fallen across the tracks long ago and made our way around the tangle of branches that left a very small opening on one side.

We had gone maybe three miles from where we had left the truck and had stopped seeing signs of life. All I could hear was the crunching of stones beneath all of our feet as we walked along. Suddenly, I heard a voice off in the distance or maybe it had been a bark. I wasn't sure with all the noise from the gravel. I hissed loud enough for everyone to hear me and we all abruptly came to a stop.

"What?" Drake asked.

"Dunno, I heard something," I answered.

"Such as?" Teddy asked.

"It sounded like a voice or a bark," I whispered. I stopped to listen and I heard something faint. "Oh shit," I said mostly to myself.

"What?" Drake asked again.

"Get me some light now," I said.

I heard him and someone else rummaging in their gear as the sound got louder. I could recognize it now, it was definitely the sound of something, scratch that some THINGS running toward us, "Hurry!" I said as I clicked the safety off on my AK.

I heard Drake flick the switch of his flashlight behind me just as Roy announced "Incoming!" The light from Drake's Maglite swung up and all I saw a flash of giant white teeth. It hit me square in the chest and knocked me to the ground. I could smell the rancid breath now and hear the snarling. It wasn't just one dog it seemed like a whole pack of five or six, it was far too dark to be sure. I did know that one was on top of me and one was gnawing on my boot.

I heard Drake get a shot off at one of them before I heard him grunt as one ran into him. I had mine held by the throat, barely an inch from my face, for the moment. Its back legs scrabbled and tried to tear me apart as it lunged at me time and again. I flailed around with my right hand trying to find my rifle but it had gotten out of reach when I fell.

"GAH, WHAT THE FUCK?" Teddy yelled. He had gotten his flashlight out and I could see the beam bouncing as he fought to keep one of the dogs at bay.

I heard two muffled shots and a quick whimper as Roy put two in one of them. He was moving quick and grabbed Drakes by the scruff of the neck yanking it off of him. Drake grabbed it by the lower jaw and I heard a quick snap as he broke its' neck. It went limp.

I pulled my right leg up away from the one by my foot and shoved my knee into the belly of the dog on top of me as I pulled out my boot knife. The dog by my feet snapped viciously at my hand but only managed to graze my thick leather glove. I thrust quickly three times up under the huge dog's ribcage, it screamed and whined as I drove it in to the hilt hoping to hit the heart. I felt the muscles in his neck go limp and the eyes rolled back as it slowly collapsed on top of me. I shoved it to the side and swung at the second dog. It looked to be a black Lab mix of some kind. It yelped and tucked his tail to run as I nicked it on a wild swing. I popped up as fast as I could to see if anyone needed help as the Lab ran off down the tracks.

Roy had helped Teddy dispatch his dog after Drake's and he was helping him up off the ground as I got there. Teddy had pulled out giant tufts of fur as he had wrestled with his and it was still gripped tight in both of his hands. He seemed unusually pale and was trembling. Later, I was told Liam had scared off two of them himself just by growling at them, not sure how much I buy it but there were no bodies around him.

"Fuckin' mutant dogs, Jesus Christ! I knew this was a shitty idea," Teddy said the clumps of fur still clenched in his fists.

"Anyone get bit?" I asked as I checked my forearm to see if it had got me.

"I don't think so boss," Tom said.

I waited for a minute to see if anyone was going to disagree with him. After I was sure no one was I looked over to see if Teddy was okay. He had dropped the fur but was now checking his arms and legs to make sure he wasn't bitten. "Teddy what's wrong?" I asked to grab his attention.

"Nothin' I'm fine," he said.

"Didn't know you were afraid of dogs," I said. "You always seem fine with Lily."

"She's different, she didn't just try and eat me," he said gathering his composure a bit more now.

"Fuck!" he swore loudly as he shook like he'd just gotten a chill up his spine. "Creepy mutant mutts," he mumbled.

"You okay now princess?" Drake asked with a grin.

"Yeah, I'm fine douchenozzle, but if I get some kind of mutant cooties from this you're the first one I'm biting," Teddy answered.

Drake started to laugh and was cut short by a scream or a howl, it was hard to tell which and it wasn't too far away. We all exchanged glances and fell back into a semblance of a formation. I shouldered my rifle and pulled one of my pistols free from the holster. Drake took point and quietly headed toward the sound.

There was a bend in the tracks and we couldn't see around the corner until we were on top of it. He had his flashlight directly underneath his pistol and I saw him take a deep breath before he stepped around the corner. He waved us on and we all inched forward behind him. The wail came again and it was closer still. I heard Roy whisper something about smoke off to the left and after a second or two I spotted it as well. It wasn't the kind made by a full fire but just the wisps from smoldering embers.

Drake nodded toward the smoke and crossed the tracks before heading down in that direction. The wail came again this time followed by the yelp of a dog. Drake glanced back at me and raised an eyebrow questioningly. I gave a shrug in return. I spotted the embers shortly after Drake. He stood straight and led with his pistol. There was a small shack almost hidden by the overgrown bushes, it'd probably been used to switch tracks back in the day.

"Coming ahead," he announced as he walked toward the dying campfire.

"Fuck you! You killed my dogs!" A shrill voice from behind a bunch of bushes said.

"They attacked us first," he said calmly, stepping slowly around them.

"Of course they did. I told them to. A man, and dog, has gotta eat don't they?" we heard the gravelly voice say.

"Listen, we don't want any trouble," Drake said as he came around the bush to see the old man already holding a large revolver pointed directly at him.

"I'd say your shit outta luck then son," he said as he cocked the hammer. He looked to be in his seventies with a scraggly grey beard and mustache. He was wearing a tattered old ski jacket, fingerless knit gloves, dirty jeans, untied, mud covered work boots and a bright orange knit cap with yellow smiley faces on it.

"This will not end well for you old man," I said as I stepped around to Drake's right.

"YOU KILLED MY FUCKING DOGS!" he screamed as he swung the 357 toward me. **"I HAVE EVERY RIGHT TO KILL AS MANY OF YOU, AS YOU TOOK FROM ME!"**

"He's right," I heard Liam say from somewhere in the back.

"Shut up!" Roy hissed.

"We can fix this," I said holding up a hand for him to wait.

"The **FUCK** you can!" he spat.

"We can, trust me," I said as I lowered my pistol in a good faith gesture.

"You got a dog with ya?" the old man asked, craning his neck to see behind us.

"No," I said with a small smile.

"Then how the **FUCK** ya gonna fix it?" he said waving his pistol.

"How bout we patch up the two injured dogs that are here and make sure you all have a little food when we leave?" I said pulling a can of beans out of my pack.

"Thatacanobeans?" he rambled quickly and dropped his pistol as he stood.

"That it is. Do we have a deal?" I asked as he almost lunged toward me.

"Yeah, yeah, as long as you have a few of these!" he said happily as he danced a little jig.

"I think we can spare a couple cans," I said with a nod.

"Good, been eating with them for the past year or so," he said pointing to the dogs who were curled up in the corner. Two of them were licking their wounds trying to clean them.

"I'm afraid to ask what they've been eating," Drake gulped.

"Here," the old man said as he tossed a can to Drake. "See for yerself."

"MMMM Alpo," Drake said showing me the very old can.

"Not fresh either," I commented.

"Ya get used to it," the old man said with a shrug before bending to toss some sticks onto his embers. "See to the dogs."

I nodded to Tom and he walked over to the shack that the dogs were lying in front of. The two unhurt dogs growled at first until the old man hissed at them. They both turned and went to sit by him at the fire. Tom approached the other two slowly and I joined him checking one while he cleaned the wound on the leg of the other. After dabbing a good bit of antibiotic on it he then wrapped it in clean gauze. The second one had been the black lab that I had cut earlier. I had caught it on the top of the head but it wasn't deep. Within a few minutes Tom had tended to both and the old man seemed happier.

We found out his name was Jacob and he lived here away from everyone because he liked dogs better than people. I started to feel bad when he had told us how he had "freed" the dogs from a kennel right after the storm had hit. There had originally been sixteen dogs and was now down to four. He sat there leaning against an old log with his hand in his pants as he told us the name and breed of every dog he had. By the time he finished the list of names his eyes had glazed over a bit and he seemed disturbingly excited.

We left some antibiotic gel with him, some extra gauze along with three cans of beans and wished him well as we made ready to head out. He broke out of his reverie long enough to thank us for the beans and quickly returned to whatever thoughts that had kept his hand in his pants the whole time. We gave a quick wave and turned to leave, I scratched the black lab behind his floppy ears on my way.

Less than a hundred yards away Drake turned to me, "Well that was certainly fuckin' creepy," he said

"Slightly," I agreed.

"So is he dating his dogs and does he at least give them a reach around?" Tom asked.

"Aw for fucks sake, I'm already not gonna be able to sleep tonight because of McCreepy back there," I grumbled.

"You wanna go back and ask him?" Teddy asked.

"Fuck no," Tom answered.

"Enough," Liam said. "Even I'm gettin' skeeved out."

We walked for a while after that in silence, trying not to think about the creepy old guy. A couple of miles down the tracks we passed what was left of the old Suffolk Downs race track. None of us would have known that it was anything beside an open field of grass and bushes if we hadn't stumbled across the old sign marking the Suffolk Downs "T" stop.

Maybe a mile later we came to the edge of what was Logan international airport. The tracks ran along the outside edge and didn't actually go into the abandoned airport. We had come across a stretch of tracks that had been washed out just after the race track. We had tried to wade through but the waves that were coming in threatened to knock us all over and into the freezing ocean. We made our way around and back onto the tracks just before getting to the airport itself. After that the path was fine and we followed them until they got to the airport train station.

Ahead of us we could see the beginning of the tunnel that would hopefully take us across into Boston proper.

Everyone seemed to be a bit sluggish so I had Drake find us a nice secluded, out of the way spot, to get a fire going and grab a few hours of sleep. I didn't know what was in the tunnel yet but I did know that I didn't want to face it half asleep.

Chapter 21

"Mack, wake up, we have a problem." Was what the whisper was saying.

"Huh?" I said as shaking the cobwebs away. "What's wrong?"

"Nothing's wrong," I heard, sitting up to see Drake and Roy seated across from me passing a bottle of Jim Beam.

"I just heard one of you whisper that we have a problem," I said scratching my head.

"No, it was 'I hope Mack brought another bottle,'" Drake said as he shook the almost empty bottle of bourbon.

"Yeah, yeah I did." I stuck out my hand so Drake would pass the bottle. "So everything's okay?" I asked after I took a swig.

"Yeah, it's been quiet. We were gonna start waking you guys in half an hour," Roy said.

"Might as well start now," I said as I stood and stretched, wincing as everything cracked and popped.

We had decided to camp in the deserted station for a few hours and grab a meal of cold canned food as well as a couple hours of sleep. We were out of the weather so it wasn't unbearably cold. There was no fire since we had no idea who was living around here or if there were patrols. We had set up a watch rotation but I still didn't want to take the chance of being snuck up on because someone saw our fire.

I packed up my gear as Roy woke the others. Drake finished off what little was in the bottom of the bottle and tossed it into a corner. Everyone was up and ready to go within a few minutes. It was still dark out as we made our way out of the station and back onto the tracks. I figured if everything worked out we should be coming out of the tunnel around dawn. We were walking in a pitch black tunnel so it didn't matter if it was light or dark outside.

It was about a three minute walk from the station to the tunnel. We all stopped at the entrance and checked our flashlights. Drake took a big gulp and started walking forward first, "I'm on point," he said before disappearing into the darkness. I put Teddy on rear guard. Roy and Tom were slightly out on our flanks. I kept Liam in the middle with me. It was a deserted old railroad tunnel. It had dirt, gravel, ties and rails, besides an occasionally maintenance door in the side of the tunnel there wasn't really anything worth looking at.

There was the slow constant sound of dripping as we walked along. Drake stopped at one point, "That dripping can't be a good thing. Where else do you get water from in an underwater tunnel?" he asked before he chuckled and continued walking.

"Well, if it was from the harbor this tunnel would've been filled years ago," I said. "Beside the occasional puddle it seems to be dry so far."

"Hope it stays that way," Drake mumbled.

The tunnel sloped downward steeply after the first hundred yards or so, which told me we were starting our descent under Boston Harbor. I tried not to think to hard about the millions of gallons over my head but somehow it kept creeping in there. I kept swinging my flashlight up to check out the tiled ceiling, as if I somehow could save myself if I knew early enough that the roof was caving in. I noticed some of the others doing it too. At least I wasn't alone in my paranoia.

I heard Drake hiss softly and held his light up to show his hand giving us the signal to stop. We all froze and waited. He walked back to me and smiled. "What's up?" I asked.

"I figured I'd let you know we were at the bottom of the hill before we start the climb up. Things can only go up from here," he said with a smirk.

We walked along quietly for about twenty minutes. Around twists and turns we went, until we heard Drake hiss again and a small splash, "Got water here," he said.

"Deep?" Roy asked.

"Nah, looks like years of runoff and bad drainage," Drake answered.

"Let's keep moving then," I said.

"Ankle," Drake said after a few feet.

"Knee," I heard him say after another ten feet.

"OOO that's cold, got shrinkage now," he said wading forward.

By that point we were all almost hip deep in the water behind him and he stopped calling out body parts, "I do not feel like swimming the rest of the way," he said.

"Let's hope it doesn't get any deeper then," I said with a shrug and pressed on. "Let's try and keep our weapons dry boys."

The water was freezing cold and got deeper the further we went. Shortly we were holding our rifles over our head and our flashlights in our mouths. Roy, who was a bit shorter than the rest of us, started swimming with one arm and held his rifle above water with the other hand.

"Hey Roy, you want me to carry you on my back?" Liam asked.

"I'm fine, it's good exercise," he said.

"I thought I was the crazy one," Liam mumbled.

I heard a whoop followed by some choice curses and sputtering, "Who was that?" I asked.

"I caught my boot on the edge of a tie, goddamn it!" Tom said.

"Did you go under?" Drake asked.

"Of course I did asshole," he answered.

"Hope your gun still works," Drake said.

"Keep it up and we'll find out," Tom grumbled.

"Thank God we brought extra clothes," I said.

I could see dry land about thirty yards away and trudged faster through the half frozen water. "I wonder if there are any white alligators in here," I heard Liam ponder as he slogged along behind me.

"There better not be!" I heard Teddy exclaim.

"They're pretty tough and live for years I hear," Liam said.

"Mack?" Teddy asked.

"There are no alligators here Teddy, relax," I said with a sigh.

"I think something just brushed past my foot," Tom said.

"Oh shit, I felt it too!"Drake yelled.

"What the fuck!" Teddy said sounding panicked

"ENOUGH!" I yelled.

"It was funny, he bought it," Tom said with a chuckle.

"Fuck you," Teddy said.

"There really could still be alligators in here though," Liam said.

"Shut up!" Teddy said.

I finally trudged up onto dry land and turned around to give the guys some light behind me. Tom looked like a drowned rat and Teddy was a bit more pale than usual. Liam just smiled as he walked by me. He dropped his pack and started to undo his pants. "You might want to wait to change," I said.

"Why?" he asked.

"There may be more water before the end of the tunnel," I answered.

"There isn't," he said and fished around in his pack for dry clothes.

"Fine," I said as I shook my head and moved down the tunnel.

Liam was correct there was no more water in the tunnel. We came to the Aquarium stop and hopped up onto the platform. We stopped for a short time to change and warm up a bit. We headed up the stairway that would lead us back into Boston proper.

We quietly made our way up the stairs of the old train station Drake and I got to the top first. We made everyone wait where they were until we took a peek outside. Drake took the left side and I took the right as we snuck to the doorway to poke our heads around the corner. "Clear," I heard Drake whisper.

"I'm clear here as well," I said scanning my side of the doorway.

It was getting brighter but everything still appeared dark and grey. We moved out of the stairwell and made our way across Atlantic Ave. A large chunk of the greenway running along Atlantic had collapsed into what were the tunnels of Rt. 93 that were created during the big dig. We were way too exposed on the street for me to be comfortable. We got to the other side of the street and ducked into a store front on the corner of State St.

After making sure we were alone we left the safety of the building and started down State St. Fifty yards ahead of us the street was covered in rubble. One of the taller buildings in this crowded area had come down either during the storm or one of the subsequent earthquakes. Drake climbed one of the larger piles of twisted concrete and steel to see if the way was clear ahead of us. He made it to the top of the pile and quickly ducked. "Shit!" he yelped. "They've got the street closed off completely."

Chapter 22

"Why are they stationed here?" Drake asked poking just the top of his head over the rubble.

"Hags and his clan are just up that street. They could be cordoning them off," Roy said.

"Especially, if they saw them gathering men and supplies," I said as making my way up to the top of the pile.

"Okay, so now what?" Drake asked as he glanced over at me.

"I'm not sure yet," I said as I flipped over onto my back. I sighed and laid my head back on the rubble. My left foot hit a loose piece of concrete and rebar sending it tumbling down the pile, causing a mini avalanche that brought other stones and crap with it.

"Uh oh!" Drake said as he quickly yanked his head down below the ridgeline.

"**HEY, YOU STOP!**" I heard from the other side as we looked at each other in fear when we both heard boots running toward us.

"**RUN!**" I yelled as I slid down the hill with a couple hundred pounds of rubble.

Drake slid down behind me, quickly passing me he took point as we ran full out to put some distance between us and the soldiers. I heard a couple of the guys behind me chuck their packs into the ruins of an old building as we ran by it. As we crossed the opening to Market St., I heard fresh footfalls and more yelling for us to stop.

They had obviously radioed ahead to the other streets. I caught a glimpse of at least three soldiers running to intercept us. **"FREEZE!"** One of them said just before I heard two shots and a grunt. I spared a second to glance over my shoulder. Liam had clocked one and saw another one fall from the shots. The third stopped to check on his friend then fell in with the three that were further behind us.

We passed what looked like it used to be a mini mall and I threw my pack into a broken storefront window. My heart was pounding and the muscles in my legs were starting to burn. "This way," Drake said huffing slightly as he peeled off to his left at the end of the mall. He cut back hard and we followed him as he turned a quick right into Faneuil Hall Market.

The two long buildings that flanked us had started to decay but they seemed to be in better shape than a lot of the newer buildings that had long since toppled.

"Left or right?" I heard Drake ask in front of me.

"Right, make sure we stay away from Hags, they're gonna have men there already," I answered as I saw him nod and pick up speed.

"They're just getting to the corner now," Liam said from the back.

"Cutting through," Drake announced as he broke hard to the right and jumped through a broken window.

Roy and I shoved our way through the door next to it. Tom followed as Teddy and Liam went through the window as well. Drake was already over the bar by the time Liam came in. Drake grunted as he plowed through a swinging door and called out that he had found the back door. I watched the rest go through and I held the swinging door waiting for Liam. He was hidden in the shadows watching the soldiers. He turned and made his way to me. "They're gonna go by us," he said as he pressed past me and went through the doorway to the kitchen.

"Go straight out and duck into the bar across the street as fast as you can," Liam said as I caught up to him on the way to the back door.

Drake shoved through the heavy metal door, checking quickly left and right before sprinting across the small street that led to the patio in front of what was a rock music bar. The awning on the front of the building was tattered and mostly gone. Drake held the heavy door while the rest of us ran into the dark building, taking up defensive positions as quickly and quietly as we could. He let the door go and hopped behind the bar steadying his rifle on the polished wood while he tried to catch his breath. It was the only wood left in the whole place. Over time I guess they had broken down the chairs and tables to use as firewood. They may have left the bar itself because it was too big or had too much polish on it, either way it made for great cover.

All I could hear was my heart pounding and everyone else's ragged breathing. We waited for what seemed like an eternity to see if this worked. "I got movement," Drake hissed.

We all held our breath as we watched the men come out from around the corner and stop. After almost a minute, two of them turned left and two ran straight, going down an alley that led away from us. We gave it another full minute before I started to hear sighs and the slumping of bodies onto the floor.

"Okay, so I guess we won't be going to see Hag's after all. I suppose we could call him with the radio," I said after I caught my breath a bit.

"No we won't," Teddy said.

"Why not?" I asked.

"Cuz we all tossed our gear during the chase," Tom answered.

I brushed back my hair and closed my eyes for a moment, "Lovely."

"So now we have no way to get in touch with George either," I said trying to clear my head.

"Pretty much," Drake said leaning against the bar.

"Does everyone at least still have their ear buds so we can talk to each other?" I asked feeling very annoyed.

"Yes," they all answered.

"I could go back and grab a couple," Teddy said.

"No, no you can't. They had to see us ditch them, they'll be expecting us to come back and get them. We've gotten all the way here I'm not gonna screw this up for gear. We still have our weapons and ammo, the rest we can live without for a day or so." I said as I pushed myself up the wall.

"We should go, in case they backtrack," I said staring out the window.

"Where to?" Drake asked as he fell in next to me at the front.

"Why don't we try and stay off of the bigger streets for a bit. We'll head up by the old clam house. Once we're clear of this area we should be okay as long as we stay away from the river.

We filed out of the bar quietly scanning the area for any sign of movement. We came out the back door and headed down the street until we came to our first left. We made the turn with Drake out front and made our way up to a street that was lined with old storefronts. I got the feeling we were being watched and kept glancing up at the boarded up windows as we went past but didn't catch anyone. We hooked a left onto Hanover Street and then a quick right onto Congress Street. We were very exposed for a couple hundred yards but it couldn't be avoided at this point. We ran the last block or so until we were under the large building at Congress and New Sudbury Street.

We stopped there for a few minutes to catch our breath and take a look around. Everything seemed quiet for the first few minutes. Then, we heard motors coming from the direction of city hall. We waited until they faded off in the distance before poking our heads out from under the overpass. We sprinted across the thirty yards of open ground and onto Canal Street. We continued silently up Canal until I could see Boston Garden in front of me. About two blocks from the last intersection we again heard the roar of an engine and hugged the side of a building. Two Humvees roared past the Garden in front of us, paying us no mind whatsoever.

I let my breath out and we all shared a worried glance before we moved ahead. As we got to the intersection of Causeway and Canal we moved into an empty bar on the corner. It had no windows left but it was dark enough inside that we wouldn't be easily spotted. After watching for a few minutes we decided to cross the huge street two at a time. We sent Roy and Liam first while we covered them from the bar.

They got across the street fine and Liam practically threw Roy over the fence that was surrounding the parking lot for the Garden. He then quickly followed Roy over. Teddy and Tom went next. They scaled the fence together and disappeared in no time. Knowing that we were still all clear Drake and I made our run for it. We hit the fence simultaneously and got to the top at almost the same time as well. Drake hopped smoothly over and as I was about to follow I snagged a boot lace on the top prong and tumbled, cursing all the way. I would have landed on my face if not for my reflexes that always seemed to get my hands out in front of me. I spent a lot of time falling or jumping off of shit as a kid so I was good at falling, not that that is actually something to be proud of. I dusted myself off and peeled back my glove to see how much damage I had done. It was only a couple of scratches but they stung like a bitch.

After letting everyone finish laughing, which took almost three minutes, I said, "We'll hold up here for a bit, it's too bright out and there are too many patrols right now."

They all agreed and we made our way inside of the beloved Boston Garden, we didn't even have to buy a ticket.

Chapter 23

It had been over a decade since I had been in the Garden. I had only been in it once after it was remodeled. It was for a concert, it was a great show and you could see the stage from every seat which was much nicer than the way it used to be. I remember that the lead singer had decided to be a diva bitch and make everyone wait for two ½ hours before he started the show. I was at that show with Drake and Anne as well.

We walked into the main stadium and I heard someone whistle behind me as we all stopped to take it in for a moment. The place was set for a basketball game. Remnants of the old parquet court were still on the floor. Someone had stolen the center tiles so the team logo was gone, but the rest was mostly intact.

We had put some chains we found around the doors to lock us in. I was going to set a watch anyway but I figured we could have a few minutes to get everyone settled in. Drake ran down and was standing on the court while Teddy and Tom took off to check out the locker rooms. Roy walked the top perimeter checking for other doors and ways in, Liam took a seat in the front row. It was dark in here except for a few holes that were over the other side of the stands.

"What kid from Boston didn't wanna do this huh?" Drake asked as he pulled up and took an imaginary jump shot from the top of the key.

"Nice form," Liam said as I put down my rifle and took off my coat next to him.

"Mack, wanna play a little imaginary one on one?" Drake asked eyes wide.

"Maybe in a few minutes," I answered.

"I think we're okay Mack," Roy said from up top. "I'll take first watch."

"Excellent and thank you," I said to Roy. He gave me a nod and disappeared out into the foyer.

I heard the heavy boots running and I glanced over to see Teddy jogging toward from the locker room holding two basketballs. "Looky what I found!" he exclaimed.

"Gimme one," Drake said holding his hands out for the pass.

Teddy tossed one over with a bounce pass as he broke off and headed to the other end to shoot around. "We okay to do this?" Teddy asked glancing over his shoulder at me.

"We should be fine. I'm betting this place is pretty soundproof. Try not to scream like a little girl too much though," I said with a grin.

"Copy that sir," he said with a smile. He nodded to Liam who popped up and jogged over toward Teddy.

I chuckled and took off my holsters before joining Drake at the other end to take a few warm up shots. I was mid jumper when I heard Tom come clunking out of the other locker room in his boots and a full uniform. I pulled up short, tucked the ball under my arm and stared in awe at him. "Whatta ya think?" he asked his arms outstretched.

The tank top was about two sizes too big and the shorts hung nearly to the ground. Tom wasn't the tallest guy in the world. "You look awesome!" I responded as I shook my head. He laughed and ran toward me. I gave him a perfect bounce pass and he went for the layup. The ball rolled delicately off his fingertips, kissed softly off the back board and into the hoop. A great shot, except for the fact that his shorts were around his ankles before he hit the ground.

"Might want to tie those tighter," Drake said laughing.

"They won't go any tighter," Tom said hiking them up. "I'm too scrawny."

We laughed and played for about an hour. It seemed like a lot less time but either way it was a nice break from the last few days. When we were done we were all sweaty and winded but felt great. Tom put his pants back on but had decided to keep the shirt beneath the one he had been wearing. Teddy relieved Roy who in turn came down and took a few minutes playing a quick game of HORSE with Drake.

It wasn't warm in here but there was no wind and it was still day-time so there was no danger of us freezing to death. "Everyone should try and get a bit of shut eye," I said after we had all wound down a bit.

"We're staying here til dark?" Roy asked.

"Yeah, should only be a few hours. Once it's good and dark we'll see if we can't find our way over to Fenway," I answered.

"I'll see if I can go find some wood for a fire," Liam said as he wandered off.

"Don't look too long, I'd rather we rest up over being warm," I said bunching my coat up as a pillow.

I have no idea how long I napped for but everyone else seemed to be out when I woke. I wandered out to the chained doors and told Tom to go get some sleep. I stood by the door for a while watching the sky darken as they day grew older. After a time I made my way back into the main arena and sat quietly in the upper row just enjoying the peace. It had been at least a week since I'd had barely a minute that someone wasn't in my face. I had responsibilities so a lot of alone time wasn't going to happen but every now and again a little bit of solitude helped clear my head. I slid down in the seat and lay my head back to be able to gaze up at the ceiling. I stared at nothing in particular for God knows how long, thinking of everything and nothing all at once.

I heard movement coming from on the floor and glanced down to see who was awake. Roy caught my eye and quietly came up to take a seat a few spots over from me. "Everything alright boss?" he asked.

"Yep, just enjoying the quiet," I said softly.

"I can leave you alone if you'd like," he said while I gave him a look and waved him off.

"Nah, I'm good," I said.

"Figured I'd offer," he said glancing down at his watch. "Figure we should give it a couple more hours before we start up again."

"Agreed," I said. It was practically pitch black in here now. If it wasn't for the hole in the roof there'd be no light at all.

"I know you said you're just enjoying the peace but you seem worried, you okay?" Roy asked.

"I just hate not knowing how things are going across the river. Not knowing has always bugged me," I answered.

"I'm sure George has it under control. We may be within range later tonight when we're a bit closer," he said.

"Yeah, I thought of that, wish we hadn't ditched the radios though, then we'd already be in range," I grumbled then paused as I thought for a moment before speaking again. "Y'know they're gonna try and turn us into some form of government if we win this don't you?" I asked as I peered over at my old friend.

"I do know that," he said nodding. "I also know they're gonna try and get you to lead part of it. Probably the military branch of it but still."

"I don't get it… I mean what the fuck? Why would you try again to do what failed so miserably the last time? Why would they think it wouldn't turn out the same way?" I asked pleading for some type of logical answer.

"Maybe it won't, in the beginning at least," Roy said with a shrug.

"Hmmm?"

"What I'm saying is that the first time it worked great for a while. It wasn't until it got corrupt and self serving that it fell apart. Maybe they feel that they can fix it and do it the right way this time, and they may be able to… for a bit," he said.

"Until it becomes corrupt again," I countered.

"That could be a very long time though," he replied.

"It could also be a very short time though," I said.

"Yep, you just never know," he said with a smile.

"Have I mentioned that I hate not knowing in the last few minutes?" I asked. He nodded as he laughed at me.

We talked quietly for a while longer. Others started to wake and get there stuff together. We pulled the chains off the door and made our way into the pitch black of night. We cautiously walked to the corner of the street and turned left. We followed this up the hill and took cover as we checked for any patrols. This would have been a much easier and faster trip if we were able to just follow Storrow Drive down to Kenmore Square. The problem with that idea though was the army had shut down everything along the Charles with patrols and Storrow is on the river.

Once we saw that the coast was clear we crossed a large open street quickly and took cover on the other side while we waited for the rest to cross. As we made our way up and over Beacon Hill we had still not seen anyone as we travelled quietly between the closely built townhouses. I occasionally smelled smoke from someone's fireplace or saw a candle lit window here and there but that was it. We came down the other side of the hill. Drake led us across the small street and into the Boston Common.

"Figured it'd be safer than walking out in the open on the streets," he said as we picked up a bit of speed while not having to worry as much about patrols.

We got to the edge of the park and crossed a street in pairs. Then we moved through what was left of the public garden and took cover in an old hotel on the corner after we crossed Arlington Street. We made our way across a couple of streets until we got to one of the many public alleys that snaked their way through the city. We could have walked straight down the street we were on and ended up in Kenmore but considering how open it was it didn't seem like the wisest of choices. The alley was smaller and unless the military was specifically looking for someone I couldn't see them patrolling these alleys often.

We still moved cautiously even in the alley. We came to the end which dumped us out near Mass. Ave. The going was much slower the closer we got to Kenmore. We started to see actual patrols even this late at night or early in the morning depending on how you wanted to look at it I suppose.

We made our way up the street that would lead us to Boylston and the backside of the park. At the corner we ran through an old gas station parking lot and down a tiny alley that ran between two buildings. We followed that until it brought us out onto Ipswich where we ran across the street, so that we were behind one of the bars on Lansdowne Street. The back door had long been busted open so we ducked inside.

We quietly made our way through the kitchen and checked through the swinging doors carefully before we walked out into the bar itself. At one time this building housed three different bars. The one on the end used to be a pool hall that had the best tables and the hottest girls bent over them. The other two bars used to change often and I never spent a lot of time in this section of town. Drunken college students were not my favorite conversationalists. The bar we were in had a baseball motif which was a good idea since it was right across a tiny street from the oldest park in the country. It had pictures, memorabilia and all kinds of equipment, bats and balls up on the walls. Some of it was signed and some of it just decoration. Most of the wooden tables and chairs were missing as well as half the bar stools. Most of the stuff on the wall was intact. Some things were just too important to some people to burn.

There was no large picture window in the front of the bar but there were windows upstairs. I had sent Teddy up about ten minutes earlier and when he came down he didn't seem happy. "On the plus side the front gate only has two guards at the moment. On the not so good side, all the lights are on and they seem to be mobilizing. They have trucks rolling out every few minutes," he said as he sat on the stairs.

"They've probably seen our troops setting up across the river. It should be getting close to dawn," I pondered.

"Got maybe an hour before sun up," Roy said checking his watch.

"Looks like we have an hour to kill then," Tom said as he came down the stairs. "I can't believe they cut doors into the green monster, fuckin' sacrilegious assholes."

Twenty minutes later the cannons started. **BOOM, BOOM, BOOM, BOOM.** Being so close to the park it was deafening. I was worried earlier about George and the men. Now with the cannons going all I could do was hope they were still safe. I had been trying since we had left the Garden to get in touch with him but it seems we still weren't close enough.

"They got the big guns goin' now huh? That should last about fifteen minutes or so to soften them up over in Cambridge," Liam said from behind me.

"Yeah, I think it's just about time for us to head out. We can use the noise to cover us getting inside… what the fuck?" I said as I turned to face Liam and saw what he had done.

"You like?" Liam asked with a little spin. He had taken his shirt off and had put on an old school catcher's mask with the matching chest protector. He was also wielding to bats like batons.

"Umm, take that shit off. This isn't the time for that," I said annoyed.

"No, I like it. Besides what's better protection for my pretty face than a catcher's mask?" he asked.

"Oh fine, I really don't actually care at this point," I said with a sigh.

"Good, cuz I wasn't taking it off," he said.

Chapter 24

"Okay, so we all know the plan correct?" I said as I gave my gear one last check.

"Yep, we go in, yada yada, kill, yada yada, don't die, yada yada, go home, that about right?" Liam asked.

"Close enough and yes we all know the plan," Drake said.

"Teddy, Roy you both okay with this?" I asked glancing over at them.

"Yeah, I'll watch Liam's back," Teddy said nodding.

"Yeah Mack, we're all good," Roy agreed.

"Alright, as long as everyone is all set we should get on it. I have a feeling it's gonna get messy very soon," I said flipping the safety off my AK.

We went out the back and moved single file down to the corner of the building. Up the street the gates were open and at the top of the street I could see two Humvees turning right to go toward the Charles. Motioning for the men to move up, we turned the corner hugging the front of the buildings. We stayed in the shadows as much as we could and made our way closer to the gates. Teddy was right, there were only two guards and they didn't seem to be paying much attention.

We stopped about twenty yards away from the nearest guard and held up waiting for our moment. It only took a couple minutes for the guns to start in again pounding the poor troops in Cambridge. **BOOM, BOOM, BOOM, BOOM** we timed our shots with the deafening roar of the cannons and the guards were taken out of the equation. We wouldn't have long but it bought us enough time for Teddy, Roy and Liam to get over there, move the bodies and duck inside.

The plan was for Roy and Teddy to stay out of sight and let Liam do his thing. They were only there in case of emergency and to wrangle him when it was time to go. I know a lot of people that would consider putting one man up against dozens of soldiers as stupid or crazy but I've seen firsthand what Liam can do when you give him free reign. I was more worried about Roy and Teddy than I was Liam.

About thirty seconds after they ducked in the gate we were in front of an employee entrance waiting for the next round of shells when I heard Liam roaring, **"WHO FUCKIN' WANTS SOME?"**

"Wow, I bet they know he's here now," Tom said just before the shelling started up again.

BOOM, BOOM, BOOM, BOOM

I nodded to him as I shot the lock and pulled the door open. "I hope he remembered to let Roy and Teddy find cover before he started."

The top of the walls had sentries walking patrols but no spotlights aimed outside to sweep the streets. They seemed to be using the existing lighting all of which pointed in toward the field. I figured that most of the troops were up on the river waiting for the shelling to stop or they were already on the other side

210

of the bridge. I never would have even considered this plan if I thought the place was fully staffed.

We ducked inside and closed the door quietly behind us. We were at the end of a long hallway that looked like it ringed the outside of the field. We could hear the commotion outside lots of yelling and screaming but no gunshots yet. Liam had weapons with him as well as the two bats. I hoped that they didn't have snipers on the wall somewhere.

"I can't believe I'm missing the show," Tom said as we quickly swept down the hallway checking the empty offices as we went.

"We shoulda told Teddy to record it," Drake joked.

"That DEFINITELY woulda been worth wasting the batteries on," I said just before we got to the corner.

We turned the corner and started checking every office in this part of the hallway. In front of us was an open door on the right hand side and we froze. A clerk stepped out with an arm full of files and moved quickly away from us without looking back. We waited until he made the turn before we moved up. I ducked into the room to make sure it was clear and heard, **"HEY, WHO'RE YOU?"** as I ran smack into another clerk with an armful of files. I took a quick breath and snapped out my arm to grab him by the back of the neck. I slammed his head off the door jamb three quick, hard times and he fell straight back as I let him go.

"You're goin soft," Tom said.

"He's not my target," I grumbled as I closed the door and headed for the next office.

The rest of the rooms were empty and we turned the next corner which led to the bullpen. I called a stop and we moved out to the doors that led out to the field. I peeked out and saw that it was clear. We made sure we were still concealed by the overhang of the stands.

Across the field I saw Liam standing near the pitcher's mound twirling the one bat he had left. He had obviously broken one of them and was using the splintered handle as more of a knife than a club. He had laid out or killed half a dozen soldiers at least and there was a wave of three more charging him as we watched.

It was over quickly. The first guy threw a roundhouse at him and Liam sidestepped to his left as he shanked the soldier with the bat handle. He fell to the side with the handle still buried in his gut while Liam spun to his right. As he moved he switched the bat to his free hand and took the second guy in the base of his skull which dropped him instantly. The third soldier tried to pull his pistol but Liam was much faster as he continued his move. He flowed out of the spin, slid the bat up under the soldiers arm pulling it straight up and away from his gun. He grabbed the fat end of the bat and clutched the soldier against his massive chest, choking him with the bat. He held him there until he either passed out or stopped breathing. I was too far away to tell which it was.

"Okay they're good for the moment. Let's get moving while the distraction is working," I said as I turned to go back inside.

"We shoulda just let him take care of this. He seems to be doing fine on his own," Tom said with a shrug as we made our way back to the hall.

"He doing exactly what he's supposed to be doing… for a change," I said as I turned right. I remembered this part of the complex. We were close to Major Burns' office. He would know where the colonel was.

There were no guards outside or near the majors' office. I listened at the door and heard a whirring sound. I assumed it was a shredder. It seemed to be standard procedure to make sure you got rid of as much as you could when your base of operations was under attack. I smiled to myself and stepped back. I was looking forward to getting a couple minutes alone with major douchebag. Tom was on one side of the door while Drake covered the other. I counted to three in my head and kicked hard at the flimsy lock. The door flew open with the first shot. They went in high and low to cover the room.

I stepped in and saw a kid no more than twenty one staring at us in terror behind the majors' desk. He had the shredder going and had dropped the paper he was about to put in it as he slowly raised his hands to surrender.

"Not exactly what I was hoping for but it should do," I mumbled.

"Please don't hurt me," the kid said as I got behind him and shoved him into the chair behind the desk.

"We won't as long as you help us," Tom said.

213

"Where's the colonel?" I asked as I paced the room.

"I dunno I'm the major's assistant I don't keep track of the colonel," he said watching me.

"Where's the major then?" Drake asked as he closed the door and leaned his back against it.

"He was on his up to the command and control center overlooking the field," he said nervously.

"The C and C is the skybox seats?" I asked.

"Skybox suites," the kid said.

"Is the colonel with the troops or is he still here," I asked again.

"I don't know," he said more forcefully. "I haven't seen him leave."

"You're not being as helpful as we'd like," Tom said as he sat on the edge of the desk and put his foot up on the seat of the office chair.

"I dunno what to tell you man, I only know what I know," the kid said. "I don't care about this shit. I just wanted fresh food and a roof over my head."

"We're gonna have to tie you up and gag you y'know?" Tom asked.

"That's fine, just don't kill me," he said nodding.

I nodded to Tom and he got to work binding the kid in the chair. Meanwhile, I leafed through the papers that were left to see if anything was worth taking. I still hadn't found anything good by the time

214

Tom finished up. We left the office empty handed and found a stairwell to take us up in the direction of the command and control center. On our way up the concrete stairs we heard gunfire coming from the direction of the field itself.

"Roy, are you guys okay?" I asked.

"We're good sir, just spotted a couple snipers they sent to the roof. I think they're running of out fodder to send out to the field," Roy replied.

"Good," I said.

At the top of the stairs we waited to make sure we didn't hear anything. After almost a minute we popped the door open and saw that the area was empty. It was a wide carpeted hallway with a great view down onto the field. I'm guessing this was the way to the skybox suites. I wasn't sure though, I never had the kind of money it takes to get a hold of those tickets. We hugged the wall and made our way down toward a closed door.

"We have no idea what's on the other side of that door do we?" Drake asked.

"Nope," I replied.

"Looks like it's show time then," Tom said as he gave me a nod.

Chapter 25

The screaming was drowned out by the rattle of automatic fire in a confined space. I watched Drake go down and Tom dive behind a couch. That left me standing in the middle of the command and control center at Fenway all alone. Across the room, less than thirty feet away, were Major Burns and three soldiers with M-16's pointing at me. Col. Jacobson was trying desperately to get to one of the radios sitting on the counter-top looking out over the field.

We had no idea what the inside of the skybox suite looked like and the sun was up now so we were out of time. Standing outside the door we decided to just bust it open and pray. I had, again done the kicking and Tom went in low while Drake went in high. As I followed them in I saw the colonel off to my right sitting at the makeshift communication console with one soldier working the radios. Before the shit hit the fan I heard the soldier passing along orders coordinating troop movements over at the river from here. Obviously, the fighting had already started.

I heard Drake swear and glanced over from the colonel. Major Burns was standing straight across from us in full combat gear with five of the colonels guards. They had heard us bust in and were all ready to counter us. Three dropped to one knee while the major and the others leveled their rifles at us. Drake opened up and tried to duck to his left. He got at least one before I saw him drop. It was all happening so fast I couldn't see where he was hit.

Tom had fired off a burst with his MP-5 and dove to his right behind a couch. He had hit a couple as well. I bolted to my left and swung my AK to the right as I unloaded in the soldier's general direction. I landed behind a coffee table and big comfy chair in the corner. I flipped the granite topped table up on its side and grabbed Drake by the collar. Dragging him behind the table with me I saw that he was breathing and conscious before I popped up to lay down a burst of suppressive fire.

"GET SOME MEN BACK HERE NOW, WE'RE BEING OVERRUN!" I heard the colonel scream into the radio.

I had seen that Tom had poked his head up from across the room and took out one standing next to the major before someone landed a burst into the back of the couch. I heard him yelp and disappear behind it again.

"TOM!" I screamed over the firing.

"I'M GOOD, JUST KILL THESE FUCKS!" he yelled back.

I took a deep breath and pushed myself up off the floor. I raised my AK to my shoulder as I stood and put a burst right into the Major's chest. He looked at me stunned and toppled backward. I swung to take aim at one of the men kneeling near him and watched in awe as the side of his face exploded before I ever pulled the trigger. A quick glance to my left showed me that Drake had pulled himself down to the end of the table and was firing around it. I swung to the next and unloaded a dozen rounds or so into the poor bastard who was taking aim at Tom. His face was covered in blood but he was back up from behind the couch as I heard the rapid fire of the smaller MP-5 tearing through the last soldier.

The communication officer had gotten caught somewhere in the crossfire and was laying face down in front of the console. I took a quick count and looked to see the colonel standing there, his face stern, weapon drawn. I pulled the trigger and heard the horrifying click of an empty magazine. I felt the blood drain out of my face and heard someone yell. I dropped my rifle and started to dive to my left while trying to pull my pistol from its harness.

I felt a burning sting in my side before I heard the report of the colonel's pistol. He pulled the trigger fast tracking me as I dove across the room, trying to tag me again. I yanked the pistol free and trained it on him. I pulled the trigger twice as I noticed he was smiling.

The first shot hit him high on the right shoulder and his arm dangled at an odd angle. The second landed square in the chest and staggered him back against the console. His back hit the plate glass window behind him and he quickly pulled himself upright. I moved in on him, firing twice more into his center of mass until I noticed that he had a Kevlar vest on, which is why the shots had seemed useless. I grabbed him by the lapels and shoved him hard up against the glass, cracking it, "I'm surrendering don't shoot!" he said, dropping his pistol. "Yeah you don't get to surrender," I said through clenched teeth.

"I'm unarmed, you wouldn't dare," he said smirking.

"Funny, I'm betting you didn't give the clan heads weapons the day you murdered them, did you?" I asked.

"But…" Was all he managed to say as I shoved my pistol up under his chin and pulled the trigger. His eyes went wide and the shot finished breaking the glass as it exited the back of his head. His now limp body fell backward with the force of the shot and started dragging me out with it.

I was taken by surprise. I couldn't seem to let go of the colonel's body as it dragged me halfway out the window. I had dropped my pistol and was bracing myself on the corner of the console, trying not to fall out. Tom was on me in a heartbeat, grabbing me by the shoulders screaming for me to let go. It sounded so far away at first but I started to focus by the third time he yelled and unclenched my fist. I watched the colonel's body fall backward and tumble through the air to finally land about 12 rows back from the field.

I was trembling and panting as I leaned forward to make sure he wasn't moving. Tom was still holding my shoulders, trying to pull me back inside. He finally pulled me in and spun me around. I saw Drake standing over one of the soldiers pulling off his fatigue shirt. He sat in the chair and started cutting the fabric with his knife.

"We need a couple quick bandages before we try and get the hell out of here," he said as he tied the first one around his bicep.

"Mack's bleeding like a stuck pig too," I heard Tom say.

I leaned against the couch and put my hand to my side. It stung like a bitch but I didn't know how bad it was until I saw all the blood on my hand. At that point I started to feel a little woozy. "Oh Jesus," was all I could manage.

"Here, use this to soak it up, and I'll toss you a strip to tie it off," he said tossing some cloth to Tom. After I was bandaged up Drake made one for Tom and he tied it like a bandana around his head. He hadn't taken a bullet to the head like I had thought. His wound had been caused by shrapnel from the couch being shot.

"We need to get the fuck out of here quickly," Drake said as we moved down the hallway, back the way we had come.

"Huh?" I asked hobbling along next to him.

"The colonel got a call out for help before we got him. This place will be crawling with troops soon," Drake said as we got to the stairwell.

"You guys okay up there?" I heard Teddy saying in my ear.

"We're on our way down now. Meet us by the bullpen," I said.

"Better hurry boss I hear engines," Teddy said.

"Get us a ride ready," Drake said.

"Already done and running but we may not have an exit in a minute or so," Roy said.

"We'll be there in under a minute," I said trying to jog.

We burst through the doors leading to the bullpen yelling for Teddy, Roy and Liam to get in the truck. The yelling quickly died as we noticed that the truck was still all the way over by the dugout. "Why didn't you bring the truck over here?" I asked leaning on Tom to hold myself up.

"We already had the truck over there when you told us to meet you here," Teddy shrugged.

"Let's go then before they show up…" I started to say but got cut off mid sentence as three Humvees came flying through the gates, followed shortly by a bunch of ground troops. They all stopped at the pitcher's mound and a line of soldiers formed in front of the Humvees.

We ducked back behind the cover of the bullpen wall and I sat there with my back against it breathing heavy, trying to think quickly. "What, you couldn't have closed the gates?" I asked glancing at Teddy.

"We were a tad busy asshole," he replied.

"We are fucked now," Tom said.

"We could always Butch and Sundance it," Liam said.

"No, I am not letting us all get killed by the Bolivian army over there. Great movie, shitty ending," I said.

From across the field you could hear one of the soldiers in the Humvee using the bull horn to tell us that we need to stand up and surrender or they would open fire in thirty seconds. Well, at least they were giving us that long.

"They definitely know where we are Mack," Roy said.

Making a run for the door behind us isn't really an option is it?" I asked.

"Not really," Tom said. "Even if one or two of us got there, they'd mow the rest of us down before we got ten feet."

"Fuck it," I said with a sigh. "Everyone got a fresh clip?"

I heard the asshole on the mound say fifteen as they all nodded at me. "No way am I lettin' him get down to 1," Drake said.

We all exchanged looks and glances as he continued to count down. At ten I nodded to Drake, we all took one final deep breath. At five we popped up from behind the wall roaring. We all pulled the trigger and screamed our throats raw. All I could hear was dozens of rifles opening fire.

Chapter 26

I stood there with my eyes still closed and noticed that my AK had stopped firing. I opened one eye slightly and snuck a peek. Drake asked "What the fuck?" next to me and I opened the other eye. All of the soldiers lay on the ground in front of us, a good thirty to forty men, dead and I had no idea how.

I lowered my rifle and leaned on the bullpen wall. I felt like I was going to fall over. My heart was pounding still. Makes sense though, I mean, seven seconds earlier I thought I'd be dead by now. That can tend to throw off a body's equilibrium. I looked down and my hands were shaking from all the adrenaline pumping through me.

"Damn, we are the baddest asses there are!" Teddy said. "You guys rock, I had my eyes closed!"

"Yeah, so did the rest of us," I said.

"Then how did we? I mean we couldn't have," Teddy stammered.

"I dunno Teddy, no fuckin' clue," I answered.

"I have an idea," Roy said pointing towards the center of the field.

Around one of the Humvees came a couple of people. At first I couldn't tell who it was. Drake and Tom raised their weapons and I pushed the muzzle of Drake's MP-5 down toward the ground. "You really wanna shoot the people that just saved our lives?" I asked him.

Hags raised a hand in greeting as he came toward us with his brother and a few friends. They were all carrying rifles and Hags had a shotgun bandolier strapped across his chest. As he got closer he burst out laughing. "You look like shit!" he said as he clamped a beefy hand on my shoulder.

"Still trying to adjust to the fact that I'm not dead," I said as I shook my head slowly.

"Yeah, you do seem a bit pale," his brother agreed.

"How the fuck?" Drake asked.

"How the fuck did we just save your asses?" Hags asked with a grin.

"Yeah that," Drake said.

"Just because you morons haven't been in contact with George doesn't mean the rest of us haven't. He told us that we should be watching for you and the timetable for the rest of the attack. When you didn't show, I figured you had probably been killed by one of the patrols that boxed us in so nicely. So, then I loaded up my men and headed for the attack site. I knew we couldn't get over the bridge into Cambridge but I figured we could at least flank them from this side. About half an hour into it I see this huge detachment break off and come runnin' this way. I said "Oh shit, maybe they are alive," and decided to follow those guys here. They were movin' so fast and there was so much noise from their Humvees that they never knew we were twenty yards behind them the whole time," he said with a shrug as if it had been no big thing.

"Well I'm glad you did. We all thought we were dead for sure," I said with a smile.

"Yeah you all looked like you were just about to shit yourselves," Hags said.

"I think I actually may have," Teddy said.

"Lovely," Drake said as he rolled his eyes.

"No time to wipe now kid. We have to go help George and the others. Did you get the colonel by the way?" Hags asked as we walked back toward the Humvee's and his sixty plus men.

"Yeah," I said quietly as I glanced up at the broken plate glass window in the skybox suite.

Hags followed my eyes and then spotted the colonels body in the stands and made a low whistling sound. "That's one problem solved. Let's get over to the river and see if we can keep George's bacon out of the fire," he said as he pulled one of the dead soldiers out of the Humvee.

"These should help a bit," Drake said as he hopped behind the machine gun mounted on the top.

"Oh yeah, we should probably get those wounds dressed on the way over as well. Don't need you guys bleeding out on us," Hags' brother said as he motioned for a man carrying a bag with a medical bag.

We took the Humvee's that the troops had shown up in and confiscated a two and a half ton that hadn't left the field to get us over to the Mass Ave. Bridge where the main battle was taking place. On the way Hag's had radioed George and told him that we were alive. George promised that we would wish we weren't when we got home. The troops were so busy with fighting and trying to get across the bridge that none of them even noticed that we rolled up behind them in their own vehicles.

That changed quickly when I jumped on the bull horn. I informed them that they were surrounded and their commanding officers had been killed. Now, most of these soldiers were volunteers and had mainly joined to give themselves and their families a better chance at staying alive. They decided that the best chance they had at seeing their families again was to quietly put down their weapons and raise their hands.

The commanding officer at the bridge called to his men that were advancing and told them to turn around. They peaceably came back to our side of the bridge and tossed their weapons in a pile on the sidewalk. They were carefully watched by Hags and his men who had commandeered several of their transports and were manning the machineguns on them.

Hags' brother gave me his radio and I let George know that he could send his men over to help secure the 300 plus soldiers that were now milling around over here. He assured me that he would get them over to us quickly and I chuckled at how long quickly could be to George. Looking around at my broken and battered team we all nodded quietly in silent agreement that it was time to go home.

The hole in my side was throbbing. Tom and Drake had just about bled through their dressings again and Liam had turned into one giant mass of bruises and cuts. He was still wearing the catcher's mask pushed up on his head. He, Roy and Teddy told us that they would stay on this side to help with the clean up for a bit. I just nodded and told them I'd see them later at home.

Me, Tom and Drake slowly started to make our way across the bridge, the other side seemed so far away now. I was limping badly and leaning on Drake slowing him down immensely. I was still in shock over being alive much less getting to go back home victorious. I'm sure we looked like chopped shit as we came up to the midway point. George had barricaded the bridge with old cars parked end to end across it, some of his men still stood behind them. Many were leaning on the hoods keeping watch.

Soldiers walked past us heading to the opposite side to drop off their weapons and await further orders. They didn't seem as upset or angry as I thought they would. One soldier split off from the group he was walking with and made his way toward the three of us. Drake saw him first and instantly pulled his pistol. The soldier stopped dead in his tracks and raised his hands. After I saw who it was I waved him forward and told Drake it was okay.

"Sorry didn't mean to spook ya," Sampson said as he got close.

"You know this guy?" Drake asked.

"He's the guy who took me down at the shop," I answered as I leaned heavily on my old friend.

"You look almost as bad as you did then," Sampson joked.

"I feel worse," I added.

"I take it you two bonded at some point?" Tom asked.

"Kinda," I replied. "What can I do for you sergeant?"

"I just wanted to let you know that once you get all of us disarmed and sent out of town. I'm gonna head home to my family. I'm done with this. I saw what the colonel was doing and it just wasn't right," he said with a shrug.

"Good to know, but I thought this was how you were taking care of your family?" I asked.

"It is, but I think I'll find a different way. We're mostly volunteers and they'll send us back down to New York anyway after this so I'll just take my leave once we get there. They'll want me to re-up but I think I'll just pass," he said.

"Well, best of luck to ya," I said with a small smile.

"Why do you think we were here?" he asked as we started to walk away.

"Excuse me?" I said.

"Why do you think we were here? The military I mean," he said.

"To get us under control," Tom answered.

"That the only reason?" Sampson asked.

"Isn't that enough?" Drake replied.

"I suppose it is, but it isn't the ONLY reason," Sampson said.

"What is then?" I asked.

"Because you're not the only group like this, you're just the most successful so far. If they can keep you all apart then you're weaker. Anyway, thanks for not killin' us all and maybe I'll see you again someday under better circumstances," he said with a sly grin as he tipped his helmet and walked off toward the other end of the bridge.

"What the fuck was all that about?" Tom asked.

"Dunno, and right this second I'm too tired to care," I said as I looked up to see George standing on the hood of a car with his black boots, black cargo pants and a black lightning bolt T-shirt that was too small for him. He was holding his rifle over his head with one hand and screaming **"WOLVERINES!"** he had a very large grin on his face.

Chapter 27

We didn't get to go home as fast as I would have liked. They took us to Mt. Auburn to get us patched up first. For Tom and Drake it was a bit easier than for me. Tom got some stitches in his forehead and a couple in his cheek. Drake's wound was a nice clean through and through. They cleaned the wound and sewed him up. My slug hadn't gone all the way through and they had to go fishing to get it out. Normally, I'd be okay with this and thankful. I don't know if Chris was just angry with me or if she was telling the truth but either way it was not a lot of fun.

She told me that they couldn't put me under for the surgery. She said they had only a limited supply and needed the anesthesia for more complex injuries. I got a couple shots of Novocain, a bottle of Jack and a leather belt to bite down on. From what I remember it hurt a fuck ton more coming out than going in, at least until I passed out. I woke up in a room later. Drake was in the bed next to me talking to Tom who was sitting in a chair in the corner.

Tom told me that Liam, Teddy and Roy had come in a couple hours ago. They had let him know that getting the troops loaded up and out of the city was going well. They figured the troops would be halfway to New York by midnight. They weren't the only troops in the whole state but they were the main fighting force and the only ones that were close. More than likely the government will send more troops soon enough but it was enough to make me smile even though my pain meds were wearing off.

Teddy and Roy hadn't really been treated they just got checked out and sent home. Liam had been kept to see if any of his massive bruising could be attributed to internal bleeding. The last anyone had heard he was still being looked at.

A little while later there was a rap on the heavy wooden door. I glanced over as George walked in. He smiled and said, "Oh good you're awake."

"For the moment anyway," I said with a weak smile.

"I'll try not to keep you long. I just wanted to check on you all and say hi as well as great work. It woulda been better if you hadn't gotten yourselves all shot up but good work none the less," he said as he sat at the end of Drake's bed.

"Everything wrap up okay?" I asked.

"Everything's fine boss, I just got a report that the troops have been loaded up and they are being transported south as we speak. Some of Hags' guys volunteered to drive the trucks to Hartford where they'll be dropped off with some food. There's a military base a few miles outside of the city. Their own people can get them where they need to go from there," he said with a grin.

"As long as it ain't back here," Drake said.

"Let's hope not," George said.

"You heading home?" I asked.

"Not yet. Need to finish up some stuff with the clan heads. I'm trying to work out some deals with our new friends while I have them all together. Gomez and I are gonna start packing up our equipment so we can go home tonight. We need to get OUR docs back to OUR clinic so we can move OUR wounded there," he said as he leaned forward on his knees and sighed.

"You alright?" Tom asked.

"Yeah, I didn't get nearly as many people killed as I thought I was. That and I'm just old and tired," he answered.

"You did great George, honestly," I said.

"We did great Mack, we all did," he said as he stood and patted me on the shoulder. "Rest up a bit and we'll have you transferred home later tonight." He smiled and waved over his shoulder as he left the room.

Fifteen minutes later a nurse came in to check on me and give me a pain pill. I didn't ask what it was I just happily swallowed it with a quick sip of water. She was a pretty girl in her early twenties and she seemed to be smiling at all three of us more than would be expected. After I took my pill she smiled again and said, "Thank you so very much, truly." She quickly left the room blushing.

"Wow she was really happy you took that pill," Drake said.

"Wonder what she woulda done if he took two for her?" Tom pondered with a smirk.

"I'm pretty sure you three are famous now," I heard Anne say from the doorway.

Lily padded across the floor toward me. She stood on her hind legs and snuffled my midsection for a full thirty second to try and figure out where I'd been. She finally came to the conclusion that it didn't really matter. She leaned in and licked the side of my face to say hello. She promptly planted herself at the foot of the bed and curled up on the floor.

"What do you mean we're famous?" Drake asked.

"I came here to check on Liam but I didn't want to leave Lily at home. As soon as I mentioned who's dog it was they fell all over themselves to get us up here," Anne said as she walked over to the bed and kissed me on the forehead before doing the same to Drake and Tom.

"Well this could be beneficial," Tom said rubbing his hands together and grinning.

"You have the gut wound right?" Anne asked as she glanced at me.

"Yeah, why?" I asked.

"I could hear a whole bunch of people talking about how they were 'So glad you were okay,' and 'How strong you were to have pulled through', among other things. So yeah, I guess you guys are famous now," she grinned evilly.

"Lovely," I said as I rolled my eyes.

"Ah enjoy it hon, you all deserve it," she said.

"How's Liam?" I asked.

"He's good, the docs are more worried about him than he or I am. They should be able to move him to our clinic tonight. They'll probably keep him for a couple days there though, just to be sure. I'm sure he's fine though, just a bit beat up," she said with a shrug.

"I told you I wouldn't get him killed," I smiled softly at her.

"Yep you did and you pulled it off. Almost got yourself killed though and that would've been almost as bad," she said as she flicked my ear.

"That was unintentional," I said rubbing my earlobe.

"I don't care what it was, that shit needs to stop. You are far too old for that shit. Besides, we need you, you can't go dying on us yet," she said.

"She is right you know," said a voice from the doorway. I looked over and Hags and Brett Twombly walked in.

"Yeah, the lady is right. You need to stop putting yourself in those kinds of spots. Your people need you too much for you to die stupidly," Hags said.

"We all need you too much for that," Brett said.

"I did what I thought needed to be done," I said defending myself.

"You did and it saved countless lives on both sides... but it was still stupid. You're a leader. You should have sent someone else. Preferably someone younger," Brett said smiling innocently.

"He is right you know... you are old," Drake said.

"Shut up," I said to Drake. "Did you guys just come by to give me crap?" I asked Brett and Hags.

"Not really, although it is fun, we actually came by to check on you all mainly," Brett said.

"Mainly?" I asked.

"We also wanted to congratulate you and maybe talk to you a bit about where we should go from here," Brett said arms folded lightly across his chest.

"Well from here I was gonna go home after they let me out of the clinic," I said sarcastically.

"Cute, but that isn't what I ..." Brett started to say.

"I know what you meant, but to be honest all I want to do at this point is get home and curl up in my little part of the world for awhile," I said.

"That may not be possible anymore," Brett said somberly.

"I realize that. That doesn't mean that I'm ready to discuss anything long term though at this moment. I know where you are Brett, I'll be sure to be in touch when I am ready," I said.

"I just hope it isn't too late by then," he said as he turned toward the door. He stopped just outside and turned, "On a side note, thank you, all of you. You did something amazing today and I'm glad you are all going to be okay," He turned again and left.

"You gonna be pissy too?" I asked as I raised an eyebrow toward Hags.

"Nahh, I was just here to check on ya. Like he said though, you guys did something no one else had the balls to do and you pulled it off. So thanks, you guys rock," he said smiling.

"I don't think I've said it yet but thank you for saving our asses. We'd have been dead without you and your men," I said.

"Glad to have helped. I'm sure I'll need your help someday too," he said with a wink. "Get some rest, me and my men are gonna head home. We'll talk soon I'm sure," he said as he left the room.

My pain meds had kicked in and I soon drifted off to a dreamless sleep. How long I was out for, I have no idea. I awoke later to find a dark room. Drake's bed was empty as was Tom's chair. Chris was sitting at the end of the bed smiling softly at me. Lily was still curled up on the floor near the foot of the bed.

"Hi," I said, it came out more of a croak.

"Hi," she said back, staring at me.

"I figured you were too mad to come see me," I said sitting up.

"You think I was mad?" she asked.

"I couldn't think of any other reason for you to not come see me," I said with a shrug.

"Well mister the world revolves around me, if you must know, I was doing my job and making sure we got everyone stable so I could get you home faster," she grinned.

"See so the world DOES revolve around me," I said excitedly.

"That is NOT what I meant and I was never mad at you. I was worried and anxious but not mad. You did what you thought you had to do. To be honest you were right. It did end things quickly and you did save lives, on both sides," she said before she leaned forward and kissed me softly.

"Wow, I was right and the world revolves around me. Maybe I didn't survive and this is heaven," I said with a smirk.

"Shut up," she said bluntly.

I chuckled and asked, "Where is everyone?"

"Everyone else is down stairs loaded up and waiting for their fearless leader so we can all go the fuck home," she said with a smile.

"You didn't wake me before now?" I asked.

"Why would I? It isn't like you can do anything except whine about wanting to leave. I figured I'd let you sleep and then get you down to the car when we were all ready," she said with a shrug.

"Do I have to stay in the clinic tonight?" I asked as I moved from the bed to the old wheelchair she had placed next to it.

"Well, I would suggest it unless you have a trained professional to keep an eye on you at your house," she said with a giggle as she wheeled me out of the room, Lily padding along behind her.

"Well there is this hot nurse I know…"

The End

7/12/12

Made in the USA
San Bernardino, CA
02 May 2013